A LOVE WORTH SEARCHING FOR

OREGON TRAIL DREAMIN' BOOK THREE

KATHLEEN BALL

Thank you to everyone who made it possible for me to get this book written. Thank you Bruce Ball, Steven Ball, Kate Springsteen Tate, Sheri McGathy, Jean Joachim and Vicki Locey.
And as always this book is dedicated to Bruce, Steven, Colt, Clara and Emmie because I love them.

CHAPTER ONE

*J*ed Todd reined in sharply and his horse skidded to a stop outside a decrepit trapper's shack. His hands shook as he vaulted to the ground and burst into the cabin. Inside were two trappers he was well acquainted with. Hinds and Shooter were the old type of trappers, good ones who didn't take too much or ruin the land; not like the newer ones, who were greedy and didn't care about the scars they left on the land. Jed cocked his brow at them and Hinds nodded toward the bedroom.

"She won't let us in. I have to leave the food outside the door." Hinds shook his head, sending the shock of dark curly hair that hung to his shoulders and the matching beard flying.

Jed's breath was caught in his throat when he went to the door and knocked. No answer came. He tapped again, a bit softer. "Lily, it's me, Jed Todd." Still there was silence. "Lily, I was on the wagon train when you were taken by the Indians. I've been searching high and low for you ever since."

"You can break the door down if you like," Shooter said. Even with his long gray hair tied neatly at his nape, he was the more fearsome looking of the two with his piercing black eyes. "We just didn't want to frighten her. You got here fast."

"I'm leading a wagon train and we happened to be at Fort Laramie when you sent word." He turned back to the door. "Lily, I need to know you're all right. Please open the door. Hinds and Shooter may look mean, but they are harmless." Jed smiled when he heard one of the men grumbling. They'd both earned their reputations by killing grizzlies. "Maybe if you just opened the door a crack I can come in there."

He wasn't sure what to do next. Thankfully, the door opened. With a sigh of relief, he stepped inside and closed the door behind him. Lily had her back against the far corner with a knife in her hand. Her expression was stony, and he was sure she'd run him through with the knife if given a reason. Her blond hair hung in two braids, and it looked as though mud was layered on it. She wore full buckskins and moccasins, and her face sported a deep scratch on the side of her neck. Anger shot through him, but he kept his expression placid.

"I'm glad you're back. I've searched and searched for you. I was beginning to give up hope and," he spread his hands, palms up, "here you are. It's so good to see you. Mike, Susan and Eli will be thrilled to hear you're safe."

"Not safe, never safe. What about my mother? Won't she be glad to have her daughter back?"

Her eyes narrowed; he couldn't tell if she was afraid or she just wanted to skin him alive. "Your mother never made it to Oregon. We buried her and said some prayers over her." Helplessness washed over him. "I'm sorry."

Her body sagged into the corner for a moment, and then she stood up straight. "You shouldn't have wasted your breath on prayers. God doesn't listen. I should know, I tried to pray for days, weeks, years but nothing."

"You're here now," Jed said gently.

"Only because I was traded for horses and animal pelts. I belong to the two men out there now." Her nostrils flared. "If they try to touch me I will kill them or die trying. I refuse to belong to anyone again." She lifted her chin up in defiance.

She had guts. He didn't see the sweet softness of the young girl he knew but she'd survived, and that was all that mattered. "You don't belong to them. They bought you for me."

Her jaw dropped. "You own me now?" Her eyes flashed with anger and pain.

"No, of course not. I just wanted you back. I can't imagine what you've been through. I wish I could have prevented your kidnapping."

"They would have killed you. I've often been glad you weren't there. They'd been tracking us for two days. A Sioux warrior named Chayton decided he needed to steal me like a prized horse. I'd thought life on the trail was harsh but it was luxury compared to how I've lived in the last few years." She glanced away and then back at him. "What are you going to do with me?" Her voice softened.

"Set you free. Make sure you're all right. I hadn't really thought past finding you. I do want you with me so I can protect you." His gaze met hers and they stared at each other for a bit. Hers was a gaze of suspicion and he hoped his was one of reassurance.

"I will not be your squaw. I will not lie with you. I'm much changed from the stupid, weak child I was. I am strong and cunning and I am a woman. Jed, perhaps you don't want to own me after all. I'm not full of shy smiles, and I don't feel any friendship in my heart for anyone. My heart has grown cold like a heavy rock on a winter's day."

Jed nodded. He'd expected crying, hysterics even, and a gratefulness to be free. She was right she was no longer the sweet child he knew. It didn't matter; he'd sworn over two years ago he'd find her and help her. He'd pictured a wonderful reunion and bringing her back to Oregon with him but now he was off kilter and wasn't as confident in his ability to help her.

"I'll do whatever I can for you. Whatever you want. Susan wants you in Oregon with her."

Lily smiled ever so briefly. "Yes, Susan is a kind woman."

"She's made my brother very happy. It's too late in the day to start out. Would you like me to heat some water for you? I bet they have a washtub you could bathe in."

Her brow furrowed. "Those two wash?"

Jed laughed. "Probably not often. I'll get the water heating. You can come and join us in the other room if you'd like."

"No, I need some time alone."

He nodded and left the room. He'd thought the hard part would be finding her, but he had a feeling the hard part was just beginning.

LILY SAT on the bed and shook her head. Jed Todd. She'd thought of him often at first but then she had pushed her old life out of her heart and refused to think of the past. It made things easier for her. A bath would be lovely, but she didn't have clean clothes to wear. She was sad about her mother, but now was not the time to mourn. She didn't have any tears anyway. Tears were a sign of weakness, and if she'd learned anything, she'd learned to be brave even if her body was shaking in fear.

He looked very handsome with his sky blue eyes and his rich soil-colored hair. He'd grown too. His shoulders were those of a man, and the mischievous look he used to wear was gone. He had a confidence he had lacked before. He'd grown into a fine man it seemed.

Jed opened the door and set the wash tub inside. "Sorry I didn't knock but this thing is heavy. I managed to find a clean towel and a bit of soap. I'll admit the soap is mine. These two don't have a sliver between them."

She smiled unintentionally and quickly stopped. "Thank you. The soap is much appreciated." Her words didn't flow as they had before. They were more halting with a pause in between them. She had learned the language of the Sioux, and the English language wasn't coming naturally —it felt foreign on her tongue. It'd get better in time, she suspected.

Jed brought in one pail of heated water after another. She wasn't sure how to act, so she kept a stony impassive look on her face. It was best to keep your feelings to yourself. A face full of expression often got slapped. She'd learned that the hard way.

"If you need anything just call," Jed said. He gave her an assessing look before he left, closing the door behind him.

She'd become suspicious of everything. She slowly walked to the water-filled tub and stared at it. What she expected to find, she didn't know. The water was clean and clear with a bit of steam rising from it. It was so inviting and she quickly took off her clothes. She stepped into the big washtub and sat down. Sitting very still, she relished the feel of the heated water.

Then, with a burst of energy, she grabbed the soap and began to wash herself. Real soap was a luxury. She scrubbed herself three times trying to get all the dirt off, and she cringed when she gazed at the scar on her thigh. It wasn't good to remember bad things. Next, she unbraided her long hair. The Sioux had made her put mud on her hair to hide the fact that she was white. She'd also had to hide whenever traders came to the village.

The water was turning black so she stood in the tub and lathered the soap in her hair then bent to rinse it. It would have to do. She stepped out and dried herself, dreading putting on her dirty buckskins. But, having no choice, she sighed as she pulled them on. Maybe someday she'd wear clothes befitting a white woman.

Jed Todd. A smile tugged at her lips knowing he was in the next room. He'd been in her dreams too often, and try as she might to be rid of him, he kept appearing. He was a familiar face. A handsome face indeed.

There was a knock on the door and she called for Jed to come in.

A slow smile spread across his face and lit his eyes.

"You look lovely. I'm so relieved to have finally found you. I'm the captain of a wagon train and I'd like to take you with me."

"You're the captain? What about Eli? Did something happen to him?"

Jed shook his head. "No, amazingly he found himself a wife. If you'd asked me before it all happened, I would have said Eli would be a bachelor for life."

"What's she like?"

"She's pretty and she has a lot of grit. She'd been beaten by people she thought were her parents, and she ended up with a limp. They tried to leave her behind at a river crossing but Eli wasn't about to let that happen. She was shy and expected to be hit but now she's a confident woman any man would be proud to have by his side."

She studied him. "You like her."

"As a sister, sure I do. Yep, my brothers did well for themselves. Both picked hard-working women. I've seen plenty of pretty women who aren't so pretty on the inside. I'm heading to Fort Laramie in the morning, and I'd be honored if you'd come with me." He stared at her until she looked away.

"*Philámayaye*, uhm...thank you. Yes, I'd like to be as a sister to you too. I'll be ready on the morn. I hope I'll be sleeping alone tonight?"

His brow furrowed. "Did Hinds or Shooter expect to sleep with you?"

"They were gentlemen. I just didn't know with you owning me and all."

"Lily, look at me. You will never have cause to be afraid of me. I promise."

Her pounding heart slowed. "I will keep you to your promise. I'm going to get some sleep. Jed, thank you for coming for me."

He grinned. "I'm just glad I didn't have to fight any Indians to get you back. Sleep well." He left the room, closing the door behind him.

Lily lay in the bed. It felt strange to sleep on something so soft. For the first time in years, she felt safe going to bed. Soon she drifted off.

———

"THAT LITTLE GAL'S been through a lot," Hinds said.

"She don't seem too far gone," Shooter noted in a grim tone. "Not like some I've seen."

"What do you mean by far gone?" Jed asked.

"Lots of times women are out of their minds by the time they're rescued. It depends on what role they played in the tribe. Some captives became slaves while others become part of a family and part of the tribe. Then there are the ones that are tortured. I'm hoping they thought Lily to be young enough to be part of a family," Shooter explained.

Jed sat down at the table and accepted a glass of whiskey. He took a big swig. "Tortured?"

"We've heard plenty from survivors. They're usually tied

and left outside for a while. Then there is the gauntlet they need to run."

"What's a gauntlet?" Jed asked.

The tribe forms two lines and they all have sticks. One by one the captives must run through and make it to the end. They're beaten with the sticks, tripped, pinched, and slapped while they run through. Those who don't make it have to run again. From what I've seen, it's very painful. Even the toughest of men fail to make it the first time. If you refuse or continue to fail your life could be forfeit." Hinds raised his arms over his head and stretched. "I think I'll get some shut-eye."

Jed and the other two men rolled out their bedrolls. Soon the cabin was filled with the sounds of the other two snoring. Jed frowned at the racket. He kept picturing Lily and hoped the transition back to the white world would be an easy one.

The next morning he was up before the sun. He made coffee and eggs and gently knocked on the bedroom door. He grasped the latch when Lily jerked it open.

"Good morning," he said. Suspicion was back in her eyes.

"Ready to go? How far are we from the fort?"

"We'll eat first, and we're about a half day's ride away from Fort Laramie. Smitty will hold the wagon train there for a few days. I told him if I didn't come back in two days to keep going and I'd catch up."

Recognition flickered in her eyes, and she nodded. "Smitty is still with you? It'll be good to see him."

"He's still with me. We hired a few new men to take Mike and Eli's places. So far the group hasn't caused any major problems, and we haven't had any incidents."

"Good. Let's eat. I want to get going as soon as possible."

After breakfast, Jed paid the trappers for the horses and livestock they'd traded for Lily. "How will you two get around without horses?"

Hinds laughed. "Let's just say that the Cavalry ain't horse savvy. The horses just end up here. Wish we had one for Lily to ride, but she's light enough you can ride double."

"That we can." He shook both men's hands and then he and Lily left the cabin. Jed tied his bedroll to the back of the saddle and mounted up. Next, he held out his arm but Lily didn't grab it. She swung herself up behind him.

"I'm ready, Jed." Those were the only words she said the whole ride. He thought about starting a conversation but she probably had a lot on her mind. He was just grateful to have finally found her. She was all in one piece and that was all that mattered. He felt her tense up when the fort came into view. Outside of the fort were numerous teepees with Indians trying to sell or trade their wares. Many of them were Sioux. He rode right on by but sighed with relief when they finally entered the fort. They'd made it.

EVERY MUSCLE in her body was on high alert. She'd recognized a few of the Sioux outside. They'd been banned from the tribe she'd been with for trying to overthrow the Chief. They should have known that the Chief had eyes and ears everywhere. He had many loyal followers. The minute he found out, he'd banished them, allowing them to take only the clothes on their backs. They were lucky he didn't have them killed.

Now inside, she remained tense. Everyone turned and stared at her and Jed, and most didn't seem friendly.

Smitty raced toward them and held out his arms to her. She easily slid down into them and was rewarded with a big hug. Smitty had always been a man of his word. Maybe her fears were for naught.

She changed her mind within the first five minutes when

people surrounded her. They wanted to know if she was Lily Lewis, the woman captured by the Indians when she'd been a child. There were even reporters from newspapers back east. They shouted so many questions at her she became dizzy. Smitty scooped her up and carried her to his wagon.

"Sorry about that, lass. Curiosity made their manners go away. You surely are a sight for sore eyes. I had my doubts we'd ever see you again, but Jed never once wavered in his belief of finding you. Heard tell you ended up with Hinders and Shooter. Those two old coots are harmless enough." He turned from her and waved his hand at the crowd. "Get away with ya!" He waited until the last of the strangers left before he turned back around. "I'll rustle up some food and coffee for you and Jed. You just rest here." He didn't wait for an answer, just hurried away.

A dark-haired man approached. "My name's Rex," he introduced himself. "I work for Jed. I'm not to bother you. I'm just supposed to protect you."

Lily gave him a curt nod and stared out the back of the wagon. Fort Laramie was like a small city. She'd been there before. It was right outside the fort's walls that Eli and Susan had been married. Her mother had stood as Susan's maid of honor. Lily's heart squeezed at the loss of her mother, so long ago but fresh for her. She needed to remember people died every day and they went to a better place.

Finally, Jed came to the wagon and motioned for her to come out. He had parcels wrapped in brown paper and tied up with string in his hand. "I did a little shopping. I know you don't have much with you." When she sat down, he handed the packages to her.

"I cannot pay you back, and it would be wrong of me to accept these from you." She tried to give the packages back.

"Actually you do have money in the bank, and you can repay me when we get to Oregon."

Money in the bank? She furrowed her brow trying to understand, but gave up and relaxed her shoulders. "Thank you." She opened the packages and by the time she was done, she wanted to cry. Jed had bought her two dresses, one green and one yellow, a nightgown, leather gloves, a shawl, a hairbrush and hairpins. The last package contained undergarments, and heat washed over her cheeks at the thought of Jeb purchasing them. She set those aside and pulled the green dress into her lap. The feel of the cotton fabric was nearly her undoing. She never thought she'd wear anything other than deerskin. "I can't thank you enough. You have thought of everything."

"I need to borrow one of your moccasins. I wanted to get you shoes but I didn't know what size. The man at the general store said to bring in your moccasin and he'd get you the right size. What else do you need?"

Before she had a chance to answer, a striking brunette linked arms with Jed and smiled up at him. "I'll tag along with you and make sure you get everything a woman needs."

Jed nodded. "Lily, this is Tara Scott. She's part of our party. Hand me your moccasin."

Lily nodded at Tara and then did as Jed asked. Jed seemed a bit clueless to Tara's intentions. There were many cunning women in the Sioux village, and she'd tangled with a few. Tara was a cunning woman, and she wanted Jed for her own. It shouldn't matter to Lily, but deep down it did.

"Thank you both. It's nice to meet you, Tara."

Tara's mouth hung open. "You speak English."

"Of course I do. I wasn't always with the Sioux." She tilted her head and stared at the other woman.

Tara turned a deep shade of red. "I don't know what I thought." She smiled up at Jed. "We'd best get going."

Jed nodded as he smiled back at Tara, "We'll be right back."

Lily watched them walking away, their heads together as they talked. Jed had a woman. She shrugged and tried to be happy for him. She climbed into the wagon and waited. A group of young kids gathered at the tailgate.

"Psst, miss? Can we ask you something?" A little towheaded boy asked.

"What did you need to know?"

"Well did you ever see them savages scalp people?" The boy's' eyes were wide.

"I've seen plenty while I was with the Sioux."

A blacked-haired girl gasped. "The Sioux are supposed to be the most brutal of all Indians. You're lucky you survived!"

"Kids come away from there. We don't know if she's tame or not." It was a woman's voice calling them away.

Tame? Had she heard correctly? She'd known there'd be questions but she never thought she'd be considered danger-ous. Her chest tightened as the children scrambled away. Surely once they got to know her, things would be different.

She was at loose ends. She always figured she'd reunite with her mother. Jed hadn't even told her how she died. This land was full of death and horrid things. She'd witnessed things she knew she'd never forget. It wasn't all that far from here that she had been captured. She hadn't known it at the time, but she was never too far from civilization. The day they took her, they traveled miles and twisted and turned their direction until she had no idea which way they traveled. She was smarter now. They taught her how to figure which way she was going using the sun.

"Those little rascals didn't hurt you did they?" Smitty asked.

She stuck her head out of the wagon. "They were just curious. Smitty, are Jed and Tara promised?"

Smitty laughed. "No, she just likes to be where ever Jed happens to be. She's a nice enough gal in small doses. Looks like they are on their way over. I'll bring you something to eat in a bit."

"Thank you, Smitty. It's nice to see a friendly face."

He reached out and gave her hand a quick squeeze. "It's more than nice to have you back."

"I see you've met, Smitty," Tara said as she approached.

"Smitty and I go way back. He held me after my father drowned. He helped my ma and me both." She shifted her gaze from the other woman to Jed. "Thank you. It'll be nice to wear regular clothes and shoes."

Tara gave her a strained smile. "Why don't we go to the river and bathe?"

All blood left Lily's face as she shook her head. "I appreciate the thought, but I can't bathe in the river."

"Certainly you won't put on new clothes. You're filthy." Tara crossed her arms in front of her talking to Lily as though she was a child.

"I've changed my mind, all thoughts are not appreciated." Lily pulled her head back into the wagon and sat with her knees pulled up to her chest. Tara's attitude was probably just a small sampling of what she'd face. As long as she was free, nothing else mattered. Lily shook her head. If Tara thought her filthy now, she should have seen her yesterday.

———

A FEW HOURS LATER, Jed carried a plate of food toward the supply wagon Lily was in. She'd been in it all day. He bet she was worn out from her ordeal. He placed the plate on a flat rock and waited by the back end of the wagon. "Lily? I brought you something to eat. The sun is going down, and it's much cooler outside."

She came to the back holding a cloth to her arm.

"What happened, sweetheart?"

"Someone stabbed me through the canvas. It's my own fault, my guard was down. I thought myself safe here." Her voice wobbled much more than she wanted.

"Come here." He gently lifted her down and sat her down onto a crate. Taking the cloth from her, he whistled. "This is a jim-dandy of a wound. Why didn't you cry out?"

"And let the enemy know my exact position? No, I lay down with a knife in my hand waiting for the coward to come in and kill me."

Jed tried to hide his annoyance. "How long ago was this?"

"An hour I think. It's hard to tell time inside the wagon."

"Did you see who it was?"

She shook her head. "No but they knew exactly where I was. I was casting a shadow I think."

Jed leaned down and scooped her up into his arms. "You are light as a feather but you don't look scrawny."

"Where are you taking me? And I'm all strong from working day and night."

Jed shifted her so her head lay on his shoulder. "Smitty will know what to do."

"I know," she whispered.

Her warm breath against his neck made his skin come alive. It was exhilarating. He walked a bit faster. She felt so good, he needed her out of his arms. He gently sat her down at Smitty's fire. He'd mistakenly thought by getting her out of his arms she'd get out from under his skin. Not true. Her scent lingered, and her hair was so soft. It was a trail he'd best not go down.

Smitty grabbed his bandages and sat down next to Lily. He exchanged a worried glance with Jed. "Let's get you fixed up. Did you see who it was?"

Lily shook her head. "I should have been more cautious. I sat leaning back against the canvas. I made myself an easy target. I can't imagine everyone is pleased I've been found.

14

Children were shooed from the wagon earlier because I might not be tame."

Anger bubbled up inside Jed. "I'm going to take a look around. I'll be back." He didn't wait for anyone to say anything but turned on his boot heel and left.

Dang it! Who would do such a thing? He'd just gotten her back. Couldn't people see that she was a victim? Couldn't they have some sympathy for all she'd been through? He found the spot where the stabber had stood. Cowboy boots had made impressions in the dirt. Judging from the size and deepness of the print, he figured the man to be bigger and heavier than him. It certainly wasn't much to go on. Besides, they were at Fort Laramie. It could have been anyone.

He took his hat off and slapped it against his thigh. Her stab wound could have been fatal. Who besides Smitty, Owen, and Rex could he trust to protect her? He'd keep his eyes open and be ready to pound the stabber into the ground.

He shook his head. She still wore her buckskins. Had he remembered to explain she'd have the wagon to herself? He certainly wasn't used to having to think about a woman's welfare. If his brothers Mike and Eli hadn't both up and married, they'd be here to give him some pointers.

A crowd had gathered around Smitty's fire, and he walked in that direction. The next thing he knew Tara was at his side. He inwardly groaned. He couldn't fathom why she thought he liked her. He'd practically scrambled his brains trying to figure out how he must have encouraged her.

"I heard Indians were in the camp trying to get Lily back," Tara said breathlessly. She must have run to catch up to him.

"No Indians. I need to go check on her." He tried to lengthen his stride, but she walked faster.

"I think it a good idea if you and I keep an eye on her."

Jed wanted to laugh. "Good with a gun, are you?"

"Well, no…"

"A bow and arrow or perhaps a knife?"

"I was brought up to be a proper lady. I have all the qualities needed to be a good wife and mother."

Jed glanced at her and nodded. "Good qualities to have if you live in Boston or New York City but out here, being good with a gun is more important." He kept walking.

"I'll look forward to you teaching me, then."

Before he had a chance to reply, he caught sight of Lily. The firelight danced across her serene features, but he bet she was anything but serene. She probably wanted to know who cut her. He finally left Tara behind as he made his way through the crowd. His gaze locked with Smitty's. Smitty nodded, and Jed felt his shoulders sag. He hadn't realized how tense they had been.

Jed sat down next to Lily and looked her over. "Are you alright? I mean besides being the center of attention."

She nodded. "Did you find the low-down coward who did this?" Her voice carried just enough for some of the people in the crowd to raise their brows.

"No." He raised his voice. "No, but there are boot tracks where the canvas was sliced. It was the doing of a white man." He heard murmurs but ignored them. He glanced around looking for anyone acting shifty, but no one caught his eye. "Come, let's get you settled. I'll stand guard over your wagon while you sleep."

Lily stood and pushed her long blond hair behind her shoulders. "I sleep with a knife so I don't think you need to bother." She wove her way through the crowd to the wagon she'd been in.

"I sleep with a knife too along with my rifle. Why don't you change into your nightclothes and get some sleep? You deserve a nice long sleep."

She gave him a sad smile and shook her head. "I haven't

really slept in over two years. Maybe I'll tell you my story someday."

Jed nodded. "I'm here for you if you need someone to talk to and not just about what happened. I like to think of us as friends."

"Friends sounds nice." She climbed up into the wagon without looking back.

He grabbed his bedroll and put it under what he now considered to be Lily's wagon. He was just grateful to have her back. That was all that mattered.

CHAPTER TWO

ily woke in the middle of the night, drenched in sweat. Nightmare after nightmare plagued her. Fortunately, she wasn't one who cried out in her sleep. She'd seen what happened to others who did. They were given something to cry out about.

So much rested on the ability to stay silent in order to thwart the enemy. She'd learned quickly in the first few days but they still gagged her when white traders came to the village. They went to great measures to hide the white prisoners from the traders and army but they didn't let them go. It didn't seem logical to her. Why keep people in camp who could bring the soldiers down upon them? The world was not a logical place.

Now she was here with Jed and a white man tried to kill her. It still made no sense. She'd grown up knowing right from wrong. Her parents had taught her the rules of polite society, but those were not the rules the Sioux followed. In fact, it was more like living with arbitrary boundaries and she never did gain enough confidence to know she was right. Being here, she hadn't expected to be attacked. That was her first mistake; she was not welcome, and she was not protected.

She pulled her sharp knife from under her pillow. She wouldn't be caught by surprise again. Killing might be frowned on, but she'd do whatever she had to for her own survival. She put her knife back under the pillow and lay back down. A pillow was such a great luxury. Listening to the sounds all around her, she smiled. Jed must have picked a rocky patch to lay his bedroll. He tossed and turned much of the night. Knowing him, he wasn't sleeping if he was guarding her.

It wasn't his fight, and she wasn't his responsibility. She'd find her own attacker and deal with him quickly. She'd learned much the last two years and killing a man was one of them.

A WHILE LATER, before the sun rose, she was up. She poured water into a basin inside of the wagon and sighed in pleasure at the bar of soap she found on a towel next to the basin. Jed was a thoughtful man. She washed up and put on her new clothes. Clothes a proper woman wore. It felt strange at first to put them on. They weren't very practical; in fact, they were thin and offered no protection against the earth's elements. But they felt nice and soft and she was grateful. He remembered lilac was her favorite color. The green dress had lilac trim around the collar.

Standing, she took a deep breath. She'd go and help Smitty make breakfast. He was always an early riser and a good soul. She was among people who knew her and that meant the world to her. The first year of her captivity, she'd hoped and prayed to be rescued. All the while she learned what she needed to do to become a useful member of the tribe. After that, she realized she was probably never leaving, and she became one of them. Their traditions and language became hers. It was very strange to speak English. She'd taught a few of the Sioux some English, but for the most part, she spoke the language of the people.

She'd been right, Smitty was squatting in front of the fire pouring himself a cup of coffee. Without missing a beat, he offered her the cup.

"Morning, Sunshine. You look mighty pretty this morning. You look rested." His wide smile warmed her heart.

"Thank you, Smitty." She took the offered cup and watched as he poured a cup for himself.

"Have a seat. This is my favorite time of the day. More often than not, there are no new troubles in the early morning. It gives me a chance to catch my breath for the day to come." He took a seat on a crate next to her. "You sure are a sight for sore eyes. It was somethin' awful the day you were taken. Jed's been stopping everywhere for two years looking for any sign of you. I'm right glad he found you. You look healthy, a bit thin perhaps but healthy."

"I'm fine, thank you. I, too, like this time of day. There is a *wolakota*…uhm…peace, peacefulness about it." It was comfortable sitting with Smitty. He didn't want or expect anything from her. "How many are in the party this time?"

"I wouldn't answer her." A tall man with a crooked mouth stepped up to the light of the fire and glared at her. "She's probably spying so she can go let the Indians know how many of us there are."

She stared at him in silence, and when Smitty moved to stand, she touched his arm. "Let it be, Smitty. There is nothing you could say that would change this man's mind. It's not worth the bother."

The stiffening she observed in the tall man was her reward. She kept her emotions to herself. It only made the man angrier, but he didn't dare lash out.

She turned her back on the man. "What are we making for breakfast? I figure since I'm taking up room in one of your wagons I'd help with all the chores. I'm used to working hard all day and well into the night, so I won't take no for an answer."

"I managed to procure eggs from the fort."

"Procure? Smitty you surprise me with your wide vocabulary." She smiled.

He turned a dull shade of red. "I'm trying to improve myself. I got me a girl back in Oregon now. I have a few things to take care of and then I'm hoping when we get back she might be interested in me."

"Any woman would be lucky to have you by her side. Who was that man?"

Smitty shook his head. "His name is Garber, and he's trouble. It's not just you. He's had his nose in everyone's business from day one."

She nodded. "At least it's just not me. Smitty, maybe I should stay at the Fort. I don't want to cause trouble, and Jed has a job to do getting his party to Oregon. I doubt most if any of the travelers want me along."

Jed walked into the circle of light. "It's not up to them. You look lovely this morning, Lily. I'd ask how well you slept but I heard you trying to be comfortable all night." He squatted down poured himself a cup of coffee and straightened up. His eyes were full of humor as he stared at her over the rim of the tin cup.

"I actually slept better than I had in a very long time. You however need to clear the area you plan to sleep on for rocks. I heard you all night long too. Besides, I have my knife. No one will get near me again. You may as well sleep in a wagon."

He smiled. "I would, but there is this cute as a button gal already using it."

Her face heated. "We'll trade tonight. You take the wagon, and I'll take the ground."

She heard laughter and turned. Tara came strolling toward them with an older version of herself.

"Good morning," Tara greeted. "Lily, this is my mother Mrs. Scott. She so wanted to meet you."

Lily nodded at the two women. "Good morning. It's very nice to meet you Mrs. Scott. I hope you enjoyed a nice respite."

Mrs. Scott's eyes widened as Tara's narrowed. Lily saw Jed's lips twitch, and she tried not to smile.

"Yes, yes we did."

"It looks to be a nice day. I'm going to earn my keep helping Smitty. If you'll excuse me, I'm sure I have water to haul. Good day, ladies." Lily stood, handed her cup to Smitty, and gave the women regal nods. Then she grabbed the pail and walked very straight-backed toward the river.

"You enjoyed that."

She stopped and turned toward Jed. "I did, and I do believe you did too. I think they expected to find a wild animal sitting at Smitty's fire. They probably thought I'd have the white women's clothes on backwards while I ate with my hands." Her smile faded. "They wouldn't have been too far off the mark if they'd have seen me a few weeks ago. My mother taught me all the social graces of society, and I haven't forgotten."

"Still spunky." Jed took the bucket from her and filled it at the river. "I know this might sound stupid but please don't go to the river alone." He held up his hand. "Let me speak. It broke my heart when you were taken, and I know you can defend yourself now, but I can't have a lump in my throat every time I see you near the water. Just for a few weeks at least. Please?"

"Of course, it's a reasonable enough request. I don't like

to bathe in the river very much but I've had no choice. My..."
She gave a dry chuckle. "...*spunk* got me through. I learned
that to survive one must be bold and daring. Tell me, how
did my mother die?"

"We believe she was killed by Big Bart. Do you remember
him?"

Pain speared her heart, and it twisted in her chest as she
nodded.

"He was desperate for another wagon. His oxen were
giving out, and he said he needed more wagons for his
whiskey. I believe he killed her."

"Then I must avenge my mother."

Jed took her hand. "She's been avenged. It turned out that
Bart had guns with him along with the whiskey. The oxen
couldn't pull them up to the higher elevations, and we left
him behind to decide how he was going to lighten his load.
The next thing we knew, he was dead, and his partner had
skedaddled back the way we came. The money you have in
the bank came from the sale of your wagon to Bart. We got
top dollar from him and Mike set up an account for you in
Oregon."

Jed's hand was large and warm. It held without intent,
surprising her with how good it felt. Somehow she'd
forgotten that not every hand hit. "I'd pictured her in Oregon
all this time. I wondered if she'd remarried. Things are so
very different from what I thought. Imagination is a strange
thing. You can imagine good things or bad." Slowly she drew
her hand out of Jed's. "We'd best get the water to Smitty."

They walked back to Smitty's wagon and all the while,
she felt someone watching her. There was a brief temptation
to tell Jed but he had enough on his mind. She could take
care of herself.

After breakfast, they packed up the wagons and Lily was
anxious to go. People from other wagon trains had taken to

staring at her every move and she had a feeling it would lead to trouble. Her instincts were right but it was the people of Jed's train that were objecting to having her along.

———

JED RAN his hand over his face and widened his stance as he stared out at the restless crowd. "Actually, now would be the time for you folks who don't want to travel with Lily to find other wagon trains. Most are going to Oregon, a few are going to California. You might not get a chance to join another for a while if you don't do it now, and traveling alone is too risky."

"Risky because of the likes of her!" Garber pointed at Lily as he shouted.

Jed took a step forward. "Lily has done nothing wrong. I, for one, feel blessed to have found her alive. I'm sure if your loved ones had been taken you'd be happy to have them back."

"I'd shoot myself before that happened!" a large woman named Wanda called out as she stepped forward. "Every woman knows to kill themselves before getting caught. Once you've been with savages, you aren't fit to live with whites. Why didn't you just shoot yourself?"

Jed opened his mouth, but Lily spoke before he could.

"I didn't have a gun. I never had access to a gun or anything else I could have killed myself with. And that doesn't matter because to me taking one's life is a mortal sin—"

"God forgives in this circumstance!" Wanda insisted.

"You don't know me. You don't know a thing about how I lived or how I survived. How dare you tell me I should have killed myself? I held on to life with the tightest of fists, and I never let go. Women like you..." She curled her lip in a sneer.

"...the weak ones, were treated very badly and they wished they were dead. That's not my story, so don't tell me what I should or shouldn't have done."

Jed admired her bold, even voice. Heck, he felt like slugging Wanda but Lily showed real restraint. She was more of a lady than Wanda would ever be. He watched as she left and walked to the oxen, probably getting ready to yoke them.

Wanda appeared speechless. But as Jed scanned the crowd, he noted she seemed to have plenty of supporters. It wasn't going to be an easy trip.

"We'll be leaving in ten minutes. Be ready." Jed turned and walked away from the people in his care. There was no such thing as a smooth trip when you were traveling over two thousand miles.

Ten minutes later he was at the front of the line yelling, "Wagons ho!"

They had about another week along the Platte River and then fifty miles of sagebrush desert. He'd have to convince people to start lightening their loads. It was never an easy job. To each person, whatever they had in their wagons was essential. They couldn't fathom parting with Aunt Sally's rocking chair, or the piano that had been in their family forever. Soon enough they'd see furniture and other treasures strewn along side of the trail from other wagon trains. And then they would be forced to face reality and make practical decisions.

Too many waited until their oxen were ready to collapse from exhaustion. It was best to prepare now. He would call a meeting tonight, and the subject of Lily would not be allowed. He'd thought there would be some silent snubbing, but Wanda's outburst that morning had him seething.

He kept an eye on everyone most of the day. Lily walked the whole way but he hadn't expected anything less. When he asked if she wanted to ride at the nooning, she simply shook her head and helped Smitty put a cold meal together. No matter how hard he tried to keep his gaze off her, it eventually landed upon her. His prayers of finding her had been answered and he felt so grateful.

"What are you grinning about?" Rex asked as he drew his bay gelding up next to Jed, on his horse Paint, named for his patchy black and white coloring.

"Just glad to have Lily back. I still can't believe I finally found her."

Rex nodded. "I feel guilty as all get out that she got stabbed. I was watching the perimeter of camp. I never suspected someone close to the wagons."

"Not your fault. We'll need to keep our eyes open. From the sound of it she can fight if she has to so she's not defenseless. Let's just hope it doesn't come to that. I appreciate you looking out for her. Meeting tonight, would you take care of informing the others?"

"I sure will," Rex said before he turned and rode down the long line of wagons.

Jed shook his head and rode to the front of the train. There were always problems but he couldn't imagine doing anything else with his life. He never planned to allow dust to collect under his feet. He had to admit he was a bit at loose ends. His focus had been so intent on finding Lily. He'd have to direct that energy in another direction. He could concentrate on being the best dang wagon train master around.

It was a long day. The weather held so they traveled about seventeen miles he estimated. The Oregon Trail was getting more crowded every year, and he found by going a few extra miles, weather permitting, they could camp where the rest weren't.

After everyone had settled and had their evening meal, he called for a meeting. It shouldn't have surprised him how many stared at Lily and she wasn't even standing with him. She was off to the side with Smitty.

"Folks, as you know we'll be traveling faster and in about a week we'll be heading into an area where water and grass are hard to come by. Most of you have some grain put by for your oxen, and we can all ration our water. My main concern is the toll it takes on the oxen. You'll need to ration the grain and water for them too. They can't continue to pull heavy wagons."

"That's why we got them oxen! They're supposed to haul our stuff all the way to Oregon!" One of the travelers named Winston Richards yelled. Jed had him pegged as a trouble-maker soon after they started the trip. He was a burly man who thought he had all the answers.

"Dead oxen pull no wagons. Lighten your loads. You'll have to before we start to ascend the mountain regions, so it might as well be now. Look your wagons over and see what you can part with. I'll be going from wagon to wagon to see if I can help. Let's get to it."

"What about the squaw?" Wanda screeched.

"Do you mean Miss Lewis?" Jed leveled Wanda with a withering stare. "I will not tolerate any slight or insult to Miss Lewis. She is a well-bred woman who has been through a terrible ordeal. She deserves our help and compassion. Meeting adjourned." He glanced at Lily, and his heart warmed at the admiration he saw in her eyes.

"Mr. Todd, I mean Jed." A blushing Jill Callen approached him. "I'd be more than happy to help Lily."

Jed smiled at the spinster. She had mousy-brown hair and dull brown eyes. Her brother was a minister, all full of fire and brimstone. As far as Jed could tell, he used Jill as an indentured servant rather than treating her as a sister. "Thank you that's very kind of you."

Jill gave him a quick nod and stared at the ground for a

moment. "I'll get to know her in the morning. Good night." She hurried toward her frowning brother without even giving Jed a second look. People would change their attitude as soon as they got to know Lily. He smiled, Jill just might be what Lily needed.

THE NEXT DAY Lily nodded for the hundredth time to something Jill had said. She surely did chatter, and Lily wasn't used to people talking so much. Her life with the Sioux had been more solitary, and words hadn't been wasted on her. She'd worked hard and done what she was told, but she'd never been invited to join in on most of their conversations.

She eventually turned a deaf ear to Jill and admired her surroundings. The world was a beautiful place, the people in it made it less than beautiful. The rushing babble and splash of the river combined with the lush rolling hills offered her soul peace. She'd learned to find it where she could.

The shoes she now wore felt odd and uncomfortable compared to her moccasins. Too bad she couldn't just pick and choose what she liked best from both the white people and the Indians. She sighed.

"Is something wrong?" Jill asked. "You know my brother wants to pray with you tonight."

"Is he having some type of religious service?"

Jill shook her head. "No, he also does one-on-one counseling with people in need of guidance. People who need to find their way back to God. I can't imagine how you lived in a Godless place for two years."

Lily's shoulders stiffened. "I thought God was everywhere. I certainly know he was with me." She walked faster to get away from Jill. Jill's brother wanted to save her soul?

Her soul was just fine. It was probably better than Jill's. They'd never stared into the eyes of the devil, but she had.

"Lily, wait! You're walking too fast! I don't want to twist an ankle."

She closed her eyes and took a deep breath. Jill was just trying to be nice. "I'm sorry, I was lost in thought." She waited for the other woman.

"Lily, I'm sorry. Of course God is everywhere, and the fact that you were able to hold onto your faith is commendable."

"Looks like we're slowing down. I'm hungry. I'd best hurry and help Smitty." She rushed off, relieved that Jill didn't try to catch up to her this time.

Smitty was already laying a fire for the nooning. Usually people ate a cold noon meal, but she remembered that Smitty almost always had a fire going. He smiled at her as she approached. "Did you enjoy walking with Jill?"

"She is a nice woman. Her brother wants to save my soul tonight I believe."

Smitty laughed. "Let me guess, she talked your ear off, and her brother thinks you're part heathen now."

Nodding she sighed. "I think his opinion is probably shared by most. Jill does tend to chatter, but I'm lucky to have someone willing to walk with me. When I was with the Sioux, I never felt as though I was truly accepted. Now here, it's the same thing. These people will never look at me as a white woman again. Most are going on to Oregon I suppose?"

"Almost all." Smitty put the coffee on to boil. He nodded and greeted a few of the travelers who came to share his fire, ringing it in coffee pots of all types.

There wasn't much conversation, and she wondered if it was because of her. They probably used to visit and have a good time. The silence was awkward and it was a relief when they took their boiled coffee and left. Smitty handed her a hoe cake and she sat down and ate it with a relish. Nothing tasted so good to her.

"Well, look at your smile!" Smitty exclaimed. "I'll make hoecakes everyday if you'll smile."

The sound of her light laughter was foreign to her, and she immediately stopped. "I've gotten out of the habit of smiling and laughing. I didn't have much occasion to do either." She wanted to frown but she kept a slight smile on her face for Smitty's sake. Her demons were her own to fight. Fight them she would. Not knowing how she fit into the world was troubling, but she'd figure it out.

Jed approached the fire, grabbed a cup, and squatted down. Nodding to them, he retrieved the coffee pot and filled his cup with steaming black liquid. "I tell ya, not one person lightened their load. They were told before we left to pack light. I know leaving things behind they think are necessary is hard, but it has to be done. One family had a heavy china cabinet that their uncle Samson made. It's just things."

"I understand what you are saying, Jed. I know you are right about the lighter loads but sometimes things are all you have to hold on to. Some people say memories will always be with you, but no matter how hard or tight you try to hold on, memories can fade until you can't capture them again. I often wished I had something of my mother's with me when I was taken by the Sioux. They wouldn't have allowed me to have it, but I wished anyway. I've forgotten the sound of her voice, and her face is hard for me to see anymore."

Heat flooded her cheeks when she realized she had a large audience listening to her. She was just a curiosity to them, and she didn't feel like being their day's entertainment. She turned and walked away from the crowded fire and went back to Jed's wagon.

"It hasn't been easy for you, has it?" Rex asked. He leaned

31

against the wagon's tailgate. "How are you at driving? Owen hurt his wrist and is having a hard time driving this wagon. I can find someone else but I wanted to ask you first."

"Thank you, Rex. I can handle the wagon and the oxen." She grabbed a jar filled with water, her sunbonnet and leather gloves, and placed them all on the front bench. After climbing up, she reached underneath to check for a rifle. It was there along with plenty of ammunition.

Watching the others get ready to go again amused her. They wasted too much energy in useless movements, and it took them a very long time to pack up. In the Indian village, she could take down and set up a teepee in a matter of minutes. It had been a necessity. Of course, it had taken her plenty of hard hits on her back from a stick before she got it right, but she always tried to be a quick learner. She had indeed been quicker than many unfortunate captives.

Jed stopped Paint next to her wagon and handed her biscuits wrapped in a bandana. "Smitty said you didn't eat."

"I did have a hoecake earlier. Thank you." She put them on the bench next to her.

"If you need to hear your mother's voice, listen to your own voice. You sound very much like her." He turned Paint and rode away.

Her heart warmed and she felt strangely comforted by his words. Soon enough she heard the words "Wagon ho!" They were off. The further they got from where the Sioux roamed the better. The sun beat down mercilessly, but the sunbonnet made a world of difference. She'd grown used to the weather extremes. Intolerable heat was much preferred to the bone freezing winters. The land they traveled through today was full of life. So much free flowing grass along with crystal-clear water. There was plenty of game if anyone had bothered to hunt. As the day grew shorter, she could see the barrenness of the land ahead. It was a big change but they'd get through it, especially with Jed leading them.

They circled the wagons and she began to unharness and unyoke the oxen. She rubbed them down with the cool grass and made sure they had plenty of water. She'd make sure they had plenty of grass to eat. Sometimes they needed a little push in the right direction toward the better grass.

She began to walk back, only to have Wanda step in her path.

"You certainly know a lot about animals. Is it because you used to be one?" Wanda laughed.

Shaking her head, Lily stopped. "We are all God's creatures."

"Except for Indians."

Lily stared at Wanda, lifted her brow and tilted her head. "God even loves the addle-brained." She heard an angry gasp as she pushed on by. This was just the start and it was already growing tiresome. Jill and Kurt Callen were waiting at her wagon. She was sorely tempted to hide, but they saw her. She slowed her pace, not eager to hear how they were going to save her soul.

"Good evening, Miss Lewis," Reverend Callen greeted.

"Good evening, Reverend, Jill. This is the last stop before barren country. I hope you are taking this time to ready your wagon and your oxen."

The reverend's face turned a slight shade of red. "The Lord will provide. Do you believe that to be so, Miss Lewis?"

"I'm still alive, aren't I? Or are you one of the people who think I should have killed myself?" She bit her lip to keep it from twitching into a smile. The reverend's jaw had dropped and he quickly closed it.

"Since you didn't, I'm afraid your soul needs my help. You have lived with the worst of heathens, and now it's time for you to come back into the fold. We should start with three hours of continuous prayer each evening and of course counseling from me."

"No need, I talk to God every day, and my soul is in no danger."

Jill's hand covered her mouth, and her brows rose. She probably wasn't used to people telling her brother no.

"There you are!" Jed exclaimed as he hooked arms with Lily. "I've been looking for you. Smitty needs some help." He turned her and started to escort her to the other wagon. He stopped and looked over his shoulder. "Nice to see you, Reverend. Have a good evening, Jill."

"Were they trying to save you from damnation?"

Her heart dropped and she halted. "Do you think I need saving?"

Jed laughed. "No, darlin' I don't. Let's go see if Smitty needs help."

"I thought you said he wanted my help."

"I saw the good reverend and his sister badgering you and decided to save you myself."

They began to walk again, and her heart lightened. If nothing else, she had Jed and Smitty in her corner.

CHAPTER THREE

The next morning Jed sat on his horse and yelled "Wagons ho!" He drank in the last sight of the Platte River and then turned Paint toward the next fifty miles of nothingness. He'd allow them to travel one more day before he demanded they lighten their wagons. They couldn't afford for oxen to start dropping along the way. Sometimes it took dire situations before people actually listened.

Things would get tense over the next week. Water would run out for those who didn't ration, and people were already worked up because of Lily. How and why he couldn't fathom. Couldn't they see it as the miracle it was? The chances of finding her had been fast heading for zero. He'd thought Jill Callen would be good for her, but her brother interfered too much. He couldn't subject Lily to the reverend anymore. He seemed to be a good man, but he had this mad gleam in his eyes when he gazed at Lily.

Not one woman asked if she needed anything. What had happened to Christian charity? He shook his head. Lily was his responsibility, and he took it seriously. If he could he'd drive the wagon with her but they needed them as light as possible. There were a few water holes up ahead mostly alkali. Some you could drink the water and some you couldn't. It was hard to distinguish. It was safer to conserve the water they had.

The train stopped on its own, and he galloped to the front of the line. The Garber wagon was the lead wagon.

"Why did you stop?" Jed asked, letting his annoyance show.

"I ain't going into that white stuff. It sure ain't snow," Garber said shaking his head.

It's alkaline. It won't hurt you to drive through it." Jed rode Paint into it to show Garber.

"Still don't look right to me. Are you sure this is the right way?" Garber squinted his eyes. "I'm all for going a different way."

"You're welcome to go to the end of the line if you like," Jed suggested growing impatient.

Garber shook his head and urged his team forward.

Jed had never had anyone just plain stop. Seven more miles, and they'd hit some good water, but it was usually crowded. He rode up and down the line, explaining they would skip the nooning in the hope of getting to the safest closest watering hole first. He'd seen wagon trains with guards circling the water and refusing to let others get to it until their people were done. Hopefully, they'd avoid all that.

Dust flew in every direction as they moved forward. The acrid smell of alkaline irritated the throat, and most folks wore bandanas covering their noses and mouths. The heavier wagons began to fall back, while the lighter ones went right around them. There was never much sympathy on the sandy plains.

It was late afternoon when they reached the water and he sighed in relief. It was deserted. He explained to the group to get what water they needed, make sure the oxen were well watered and to fill a tub and move away from the watering hole. They'd wash if they needed to but they needed to make room at the hole for any other travelers who might arrive.

They circled about a mile away, which gave them plenty of time to rest the oxen and get ready for the night. Once again, he went from wagon to wagon, this time demanding that people leave behind heavy objects. He'd leave them behind if their oxen died because of their stupidity.

After his rounds, he spotted Lily smiling at him. When she saw him watching she quickly took her smile away but he went to her anyway.

"What's so funny?"

"You. These people give you so much grief for non-essentials. They don't know what it's like to travel constantly with everything you own on your back. There are times I think the Sioux are far smarter than some of these white men."

Jed turned when he heard a gasp. Tara Scott stood with her eyes wide and her hand over her mouth. She shook her head and pointed at Lily. "Some say you are too far gone to be allowed around whites. I've heard rumors you were married and had a baby while you were with them. I really thought since you were Jed's friend it wasn't true. But now I know you have nothing but disdain for those of us in this wagon party. I'll be sure to sleep with my gun under my pillow from now on!"

Lily turned white, and her hand started to tremble. He gently took her hand in his. "Tara, I think that's enough. The rumors aren't true, and I have been searching for Lily for over two years. She is one of the finest young ladies I know."

"You either need a new set of ladies to know or glasses because she is certainly no lady! She's a dirty rotten—"

Jed took a step forward. "Don't say anything you'll regret.

Now, we were having a private conversation when you rudely eavesdropped on us. Go back to your wagon."

From the fire in her eyes, he knew there was going to be trouble. He gave Lily's hand a gentle squeeze before he let go.

"You don't need to protect me, Jed. I can see it will cost you your job. I'm not worth it." She turned to walk away.

Jed gently grabbed her shoulders and turned her toward him. "You are worth it. You are a glorious woman. Don't let others take that away from you."

Her blue eyes flashed. "Don't you want to know if it's true? Aren't you dying to know if I have a child?"

His heart squeezed at the pain in her eyes. "Honey, your happiness is all that matters. You don't have to tell me a thing, and I won't question. I'm so grateful to have you here. If you wanted to drink your water out of a boot I'd still like you."

She smiled. "Water out of a boot? You've done that, haven't you?"

"Desperate times. It was a good idea at the time." He gave her his best grin and was warmed when she smiled back.

"Jed? I was never married, and I don't have a child. I don't care what the others think. I just want to be truthful with you."

Pulling her into his arms felt like a homecoming. It felt so right, and he wanted it to last, but he wanted to kiss her, and that he couldn't do. She was in no state to know her own heart or mind. In her eyes, he was her rescuer, her hero. He smiled, he wasn't a hero. He didn't look for her for heroics. It was for a selfish reason; he cared about her. He slowly let go and took a step back. "I'll rig up something so you can bathe in privacy. It's going to be a long dry haul from here. Then I need to lighten some wagons."

"Thank you, Jed." She turned and walked away.

THE NEXT MORNING the sun was barely making itself known when Lily woke. She quickly dressed and took a deep breath. It'd been a noisy night. The other wagon train played music and the people were loud, but that wasn't what bothered her the most. It was the small sounds she heard near her wagon. Someone lingered near until Jed went to bed. It had been a late night for him. She'd heard the protests and tears as he made people pull the heavy furniture out of their wagons.

She might have felt that way before but not now. Those people would be surprised at how little they actually needed. She sat and listened. Birds were chirping but there was something else. She sensed that someone was watching the wagon again. She drew her knife and hopped out the back, landing in a squatted position. She quickly turned in a circle but she saw no one, except for Jed, who was still sleeping under the wagon. It was strange. There weren't any trees on the barren earth they camped on. There was nowhere to hide.

She cautiously walked to Smitty, who was already drinking coffee. He looked around too as though he also felt it. They both turned in the direction of the other wagon train at the same time and saw the men from that train start running toward them with guns in their hands. Smitty grabbed a metal triangle from the back of his wagon and made it ring with a metal baton. It clanged loud and clear. Meanwhile, she ran, got Jed up, and grabbed her rifle while yelling for everyone to wake up, they were about to be attacked.

Men barreled over the back end of their wagons, guns in their hands and stared at each other. Thankfully, Jed and Smitty got them all pointed in the right direction. Women screamed and children cried. Lily tried to get most of them to hide under their wagons, but some thought she was trying to trick them. Finally, she slid under a wagon and got ready to shoot.

The group from the other train was shocked by the preparedness of Jeb's group so they backed off. Jed instructed everyone to hold their fire. It seemed as though most held their breath too. The other men turned and ran away. Lily rested her forehead on her arms and thanked God. She lay under the wagon for a bit, feeling drained. When she wiggled her way out, she was surprised to see fingers pointed in her direction.

Wanda took a step forward. "She tried to get me killed. She told me to stay in my wagon. Everyone knows to get under the wagon in an attack!"

It was as though someone had slapped her in the face. What was wrong with these people? Hadn't she and Smitty saved their lives? Disgusted, she pushed her way through the crowd and went to Smitty's wagon and crawled inside. She didn't feel safe in her wagon.

It wouldn't matter how helpful or good she was, they'd never accept her. Up until now, she'd really thought it was just a matter of time. Once they got to know her, they'd like her. But they'd rather she had never been rescued. Several had been very vocal about their dislike, and she had thought it was only those people. But it was just about everyone. She saw it on their faces, and her heart shattered. With the Sioux, she'd had to be emotionless, hard and brave. She couldn't let down her guard for one minute, and somehow here she'd forgotten to keep herself isolated and to protect her feelings. Why couldn't she be herself? She shook her head as tears flowed. She didn't even know who she was anymore. She did know one thing, no matter who they were, people still wouldn't accept her.

It seemed like forever before Jed climbed in after her. She

was starting to feel guilty that she should be helping Smitty. She wasn't as fearless as she'd thought. She just couldn't face the crowd.

He climbed in, took one look at her, and immediately took her into his arms, tucking her head under his chin. It was the most comforting hug she could remember ever having. Wrapping both arms around him, she held on, and finally she wept.

She wept for her lost childhood, the loss of her mother and for being captured. She cried that deep down she knew she was no longer good enough for Jed or any other man. Finally, she wept for all her trials and tribulations that only she knew about. The fear and the terror she'd faced would be forever seared in her soul.

It was as though she'd been waiting for over two years to be held and made to feel safe. He was such a good man he deserved an untainted wife. He'd have a family of his own while she… Her shoulders sagged. It was too much to think about. She was a survivor, she'd get through. Perhaps she'd move to the Great Pacific Northwest. She'd heard it was sparsely populated. It would be a good place to start over.

"Have you ever heard of the Pacific Northwest?" She felt him nod.

"Why do you ask?"

"I don't know. I heard a person can travel for days without seeing another person. It appeals to me. Is it far from Oregon?"

"It's starts in the Washington territory and goes on up the coast of Canada."

"Washington is not in the West and it is not on the Pacific Coast. I'm not stupid you know."

Jed gave her a gentle squeeze. "I know you're not stupid. Washington Territory is not a part of Washington where the president lives. In fact, you're right about it being unpopulated in many parts of it. I heard the trees are so tall you have to lay on your back to see the tops. There are Indians up there too. If you're worried about where you'll go, you are welcome to make your home on my family's ranch."

Swallowing hard she nodded. He had enough to worry about getting them all to Oregon without having to worry about her. She'd stand like a warrior from now on and fight her own battles. "I need to help Smitty."

He slowly let her go and then he cupped her cheeks in the palms of his hands. "You will be just fine." He leaned in and kissed her on the forehead, and before she could even respond, he was gone. He was a good man.

With a lump in her throat, she climbed out of the wagon and dove right into helping Smitty. He liked to make a couple batches of biscuits each morning and hand them out to the kids during the day. He said that when supplies dwindled the kids suffered the most. His heart was good and pure.

They worked in comfortable silence for a while. Then Smitty handed her a cup of coffee, poured one for himself, and gestured for her to sit down. "We never did have our morning quiet time. You sure were quick on your feet, and you saved many lives."

Her face heated. "You warned the folks."

He nodded. "I did clang the triangle." He laughed. "Seriously though, I had a feeling but it wasn't strong enough, and I knew Indians didn't like this part of the country. Your instincts tipped me off. Funny how people are always quick to blame and slow to praise. I want you to know I am grateful to you. Most of those women would have been killed. I've heard of it happening a time or two, but never thought it would happen to us."

"Why would one wagon party attack another?"

"The truth is they aren't going to Oregon. Usually you have to be on guard right out of Independence, Missouri.

Lots of wagon trains get robbed by people who pretend to be on a train. They don't usually come out this far. Why bother when there are easy pickings closer to towns?"

"That would make more sense. Or at least before people lighten their wagons."

Jed joined them, hunkered down, and poured himself some coffee. "I've been thinking the same thing. Have you noticed anyone suspicious in our party?"

Smitty shook his head. "No one shifty. If someone is carrying something of value, they're keeping a low profile. I guess it's time to make friends with the unfriendly."

"The unfriendly?" she asked.

Smitty smiled. "You know, the ones that keep to themselves. In a case like this, I'd rule out the mean ones and the busybodies."

Jed took a swig of his coffee. "Too bad we didn't capture one."

She laughed. "I've seen many interrogation techniques you've probably never heard of."

They all turned toward the sound of a throat clearing. Winston Richards stood there, stone faced. "A word of advice, Miss Lewis. Don't be caught saying things like that. People are already on edge with you traveling with us. You don't need to talk about your savage ways."

"Pa, stop. Let's just go back to our wagon," Ricky Richards said. He sent her an apologetic look.

"Ricky, I know you're sweet on her and all, but this is exactly why you have to give up your ridiculous notion of her. Once a woman had gone savage there is no redeeming her." Winston shook his head.

For a moment, she wanted to slap him. She put her hand to her throat. Why had that even popped into her head?

Jed stepped in front of her, and widened his stance. "I think this conversation is done, don't you think, Winston?"

Winston scowled while Ricky frowned.

"Come on son. Let's get ready to go."

She sagged onto a crate and put her coffee down. Staring at the dry ground, she wondered what had come over her. Perhaps she needed to start questioning her sanity. Lots of captives went crazy. Was that what was happening to her? Looking up her gaze met Jed's questioning one. She gave him a slight smile hoping he'd think everything was fine.

"I'd best check on the biscuits. No one likes them burned." She could feel the gazes of both men upon her. Dang, even Smitty thinks there's something wrong.

Rex rode in and slid off his horse. "I followed them. They went back the way they came. I sure wish we'd have captured one of them."

She couldn't help the laugh that bubbled from her. "It's better this way, believe me, Rex."

JED SHOOK his head as he rode Paint up and down the line of wagons all day. It certainly had been a jam-packed day. Conspiracy theories were related to him all day. Half thought those men worked with the Indians and hence, Lily. A few thought Lily had snuck over to the other party and enticed them to come and raid the camp with promises of riches. The other half of the people knew it was the greed of men and were busy watching the horizon for more trouble.

Wanda demanded a vote to kick Lily off the train. And according to Wanda, Lily would be just fine with her *Indian knowhow*. It always amazed him that a group with the common goal of reaching Oregon could all be so vastly different. More than likely they'd be neighbors out there, why not become friendly along the way. The smarter families did just that. They cooked together, watched each other's kids, washed clothes together. Men hunted together and sat around their fires telling stories. They would be the ones who would make it out west.

Though he went back east the beginning of each year, he refused to escort anyone back to Independence. It was always the people who gave him a hard time who asked him to take them. Plus it would take too long. They traveled light and bought new wagons and supplies in Missouri each year.

They decided to skip the nooning and keep going well into the night so they could get to the next watering hole that much sooner. Tomorrow, they'd find water and let the oxen have a nice long rest.

He, too, watched the horizon. Not expecting more trouble but the attack this morning didn't sit well. If they'd been that determined this morning, he was certain they'd be back. He needed to find out what was going on. Too many people were already wound up about Lily, and they were placing the blame at her feet.

He'd been amazed when he saw her jump from the wagon this morning. He'd been awake, just waiting for the sun to begin to rise before he got up. The way she landed on her feet and crouched down with her knife extended as she made a wide circle. He'd been both impressed and confused. He hadn't heard anything near the wagon. He was getting ready to roll out from under the wagon when she came running.

He'd never forget the incredible sight of her running from wagon to wagon with her long blond hair blowing in the wind behind her. If anyone should be put off the train, it should be Wanda for her false accusations. Who knew how many men they would have lost this morning if not for her. Why was she talking about Washington Territory? Surely now that he found her, she wouldn't leave and go so far from him. She wouldn't, would she?

Confound it! She'd become such a big part of his life

while she was gone, and he never expected her to take an even bigger part when he found her. He never thought any further than finding her. Now what? He wasn't any good at this relationship thing. Women found him attractive and a few had trifled with his feelings. He'd been told he wore his heart on his sleeve and it allowed women to lead him on.

Lily didn't seem the type but he didn't want to open his heart to any woman. He hadn't fully expected that she be such a part of him. He felt so fiercely about protecting her he'd kill or die for her and that scared him.

He wanted to know more about her time with the Sioux but he'd wait until she told him. Too many people expected her to spill her story to them and he could see her dismay when anyone asked her questions. He was grateful she was whole and healthy.

It was his turn to ask the people he was leading some questions. Someone had to know why they had been attacked. But no one jumped out at him, and he didn't have a notion where to begin. He'd been watching the wagons and none were leaving deep ruts indicating they were extraordinarily heavy. Most wagons had a second floor built on top of the bottom with room in between the layers for extra food storage. No one was carrying bars of gold that much he knew.

He took off his hat and wiped his brow with his sleeve. It was a hot one, and the smell of the alkali was nauseating. There were a few women in the family way. He'd need to go and check to see how they were faring. As he rode and chatted with each driver, he looked for clues. The only thing unusual was the fine wagon the reverend and his sister had. Their clothes didn't indicate the same level of wealth as their wagon. It wasn't a very good clue. His congregation could have purchased the wagon for them. Plus he wasn't exactly lying low. No, Jed would need to keep his eyes open.

A piercing scream filled the air, and the wagons came to a halt. Jed raced toward the front of the line and his heart sank. A small child lay in one of the ruts, having been crushed beneath a wagon wheel. Blood pooled around her body. Matilda, he recalled her name. Her mother, Sally Smathers, sat next to her dead daughter cradling her head in her lap while her husband, Big Tim, looked on helplessly.

Sally glared at Winston Richards. "This is your fault! How could you run over my baby?" Tears ran down her face.

Winston turned white. "I didn't see her. I thought she was in the back of your wagon. She'd been in there most of the day. She waved at me several times. I'm so sorry."

Terrance, Matilda's five-year-old brother took a step forward. "She was. She decided to jump out the back so she could walk. I tried to stop her but she called me a baby. She jumped and then she screamed when an oxen plowed over her and now she's dead."

"It's his fault!" Sally pointed at Winston. "He could have stopped his oxen. Now my Matilda is gone." A fresh round of weeping began.

Big Tim shook his head as he crouched down next to Sally. "You know we told her again and again not to jump out the back. There is no way Winston could have stopped in time. It was a tragic accident. We need to bury our girl and make sure proper prayers are said for her." He took Matilda into his arms and carried her to the side of the trail.

Jed, Smitty and Rex all grabbed shovels and began to dig a grave. This type of thing was far too common. More people died of accidents than sickness on most trains.

The reverend led a service at the graveside, and then Big Tim led Sally and Terrence back to their wagon. Jed gave them the option of stopping for the night, but they wanted to go on. The wagons behind the grave made sure to run over it with their wheels. Mostly to make sure the dirt was hard packed and animals couldn't dig up the body and of course, there were those who believed that Indians dug up the graves looking for anything they could take from the bodies.

When they did stop, the mood was somber. Everyone went about their chores without much chatter. Things were settling down for the night when another scream filled the air. Jed ran toward Winston's wagon. Winston was bleeding from his shoulder, and Rex was holding Sally back. A long knife lay on the ground.

Smitty appeared as if by magic with his doctoring kit, and Big Tim escorted his wife away to their wagon. He apologized profusely for his wife's actions.

"I suppose there will be a hanging come morning?" Winston asked. He winced. Smitty mustn't have been as gentle sewing Winston up after that question.

Jed shook his head. "I don't think so. She's out of her mind with grief. I'll have Big Tim keep her in his sight at all times."

"Now see here! She tried to kill me. What if she got Ricky instead? She's too dangerous to have on our wagon train and I want justice."

Jed sighed. "Let's just sleep on it and talk more in the morning. Clearer heads might make better decisions."

Winston growled. "I hope this means you'll realize what really needs to be done."

"Jed, why don't you get these onlookers off to their wagons, and I'll finish stitching up Winston here?" Smitty gave him a knowing nod. It was best to get things under control as quickly as possible.

Jed and Rex got the crowd to scatter.

Smitty finally came back to his fire and shook his head. "Don't worry I stuck him extra hard with the needle. How anyone can be so all-fire mean is beyond me. He's just lucky she didn't kill him." He paused and drew a deep breath then leveled his gaze on Jed. "Sally does need to be watched."

Jed nodded. "I agree, she's dangerous, but I'm not hanging anyone. I'd best get some shuteye." He stood, raising his arms over his head in a stretch before he walked away.

He was surprised to see Tara standing not too far from his wagon. She did know Lily slept inside, didn't she?

"I need to talk to you, Jed," she whispered. "You need to get rid of that Indian you have in your wagon. Nothing good can come from it. I really think you need to heed my warning. I've heard people talking about stringing *her* up instead of Sally."

He furrowed his brow. "That doesn't make any sense."

"They want blood, but not necessarily Sally's." She looked furtively around then lowered her voice. "Just send her on her way tonight."

"Tara, I'm not sending her away, now or ever. You need to come to terms with it. We all just need to work together and get to Oregon where everyone can start new lives. Let me walk you back to your wagon."

She crossed her arms in front of her and shook her head. "I can get there myself. I don't need anything from you anymore." She turned on her heel, and he watched her until she was safe at her wagon.

"I'm sorry I cost you your friendship," Lily whispered from the back of the wagon.

"She'll cool off. I'm going to sleep in the wagon tonight. I don't trust half these people and they are thirsty for blood or something. I'll sit at the back here while you sleep."

"You're too good to me," she said before she popped her head back into the wagon.

He waited a few minutes for her to get settled before he rolled some blankets and put them under the wagon, hoping it looked like him sleeping under there. Then he climbed in.

It was pretty dark except for the bit of moonlight that caught the side of her face. She'd grown into a beautiful woman. There was such a difference from two years ago. Gone were the shy smiles, and instead she had the look of a woman who knew too much of life. Her innocence and naivety were gone. Sadness washed over him at the thought.

"Good night, Jed, and thanks for not letting them stretch my neck." There was the slightest hint of humor in her voice.

"Good night." He had a feeling she'd never allow anyone to get the jump on her again. She was never in any fear of hanging. He shook his head. She was one heck of a woman. He closed his eyes. It was going to be a trying morning.

CHAPTER FOUR

he foliage ahead had Lily smiling. It had been almost three weeks that they'd been traveling the wasteland. Tempers flew as well as accusations. The so-called good people of the wagon train weren't above stealing a cup of water out of their neighbor's barrels.

The Smathers' had been riding lead since the incident, and Winston had been riding in the back so he could keep an eye on Sally. Lily had tried to make herself as scarce as possible those first few days after the stabbing. It was a bit lonely, spending each day by herself. She even missed Jill's non stop prattling. Thank goodness for Smitty, Jed, Owen and Rex. At least they spent time with her each morning and night.

At one point, she tried to show the travelers that keeping a small stone in their mouths would keep them from being so dry. Obviously, it was a trick to kill them all. She knew of plenty of ways to conserve water, but they didn't want her advice. They'd rather suffer, she guessed.

She shook her head. She'd shot down a few birds but no one wanted any of the meat except for Smitty, Jed, Owen and

Rex. Fools, all of them. Mostly it was the husbands. The women looked longingly at the meal she prepared and with enough rice and beans, she could have stretched the meal to feed many.

"Lost in thought?"

Startled, she turned and saw Jed riding beside her wagon. "Is that Independence Rock?"

"It sure is. We should hit it by nightfall."

She smiled. "It's so much bigger than I ever imagined."

"It's huge all right. I've been hoping that you'd be able to etch your name on it someday. It's a miracle that you'll be able to do it." He seemed to grow solemn for a while. "I hope you'll allow me to climb it with you."

Her body flooded with warmth. "I wouldn't have it any other way. So, what happened this morning with the Smathers'?"

"Sally took an axe and smashed their water barrel until all their water was gone. The poor thing has her hands tied inside the wagon so she doesn't hurt herself."

"Grief makes people do all kinds of things." She could still hear the mournful wails of the Sioux when they lost someone. They also cut themselves. It was hard to watch and even harder to partake in.

"Winston keeps giving me an, *I told you* stare. I'm ignoring it. There will be plenty of wagons at the rock, so please be careful." His eyes were so full of caring she almost felt loved.

"Of course I will. Don't worry I won't try to teach them any Indian dances."

He grinned and shook his head. "You have the oddest sense of humor."

"Sometimes you have to make a choice. You can either laugh or cry. Crying could have been a death sentence for me."

"I'm glad you didn't cry. I can't wait for our climb. I'd best keep riding." He tipped his hat and spurred Paint.

She'd rather gaze at him than at the beautiful lush scenery they were entering. Somehow, he made her feel whole in a way she didn't understand. Could the right man make a woman feel complete? Was that why people married and had children? There was so much she wished she knew. Once more, she ached for the loss of her mother.

The oxen moved faster as they approached the river. They were just as hot and thirsty as the rest. It took a bit more muscle to keep them at an even keel. Finally they made it and circled. Looking up at the rock, she felt so tiny.

After taking care of the oxen, she made her way to Smitty's fire. She thought she'd be used to the whispers, but she wasn't, yet no one would even know she heard. She held her head up high and continued walking.

A large sharp rock hit her head and she almost cried out. It hurt like the dickens, and when she touched her forehead, her fingers came away sticky with blood.

"Go back to where you came from!" The voice sounded like a young man, but she didn't look to see. She kept walking.

Blood ran down her face. The rock hadn't seemed to be big enough to cause so much blood. She had almost gotten to Smitty's when he jumped up and ran to her. He swept her up and placed her on one of the crates.

"What happened to you?" The concern in his voice touched her.

"Someone threw a rock at me. It's bleeding much more than it hurts."

Smitty handed her a clean cloth and she held it against her wound.

"Head wounds tend to bleed more," he explained. "Did you see who did it?"

"No, I was trying to ignore all the jests about me as I walked over here. Not one person offered to help. What has happened to people? My mother would have helped anyone in need. Have people changed so much in the last few years?"

Smitty took the cloth and wet it. He washed off a good amount of blood. "I don't think you'll need to be stitched but you should keep it bandaged. Your mother was a wonderful kindhearted woman. There are still a few out there like her, but she was a rare person of considerable compassion."

He walked to the back of his wagon and pulled out strips of cloth. "Let's get you fixed up."

Before he had a chance to reach her, Jed walked toward her, and his jaw dropped.

"Did you fall?" He knelt down next to her.

"No, I didn't fall."

"Someone threw a rock at her. Got her pretty good too," Smitty said.

"Did—"

"Nope," Smitty interrupted. "She didn't see who did it. I say we roust the men and question them."

"I believe it to be a younger man or older boy. I did hear his voice. Just let it be. I don't want to give people more reason to hate me." She sat very still as Smitty wrapped her head. A wave of nausea hit her, but she wasn't about to give in to it. "I'll be fine. Besides I have a date to climb Independence Rock."

She noticed the look Smitty and Jed exchanged. They weren't going to let it go. Men were like that, she supposed. She remembered another time in her life when rocks were thrown at her. When she first arrived at the Sioux Village, Chayton the man who kidnapped her, dropped the rope he had around her neck and hands and left her there to be beaten with sticks and hit by rocks. At the time, she had curled into a ball and protected her head.

Later, she realized they did that to each new captive. She never understood why. Now thinking about it, they probably wanted the captive to know who was in charge. She doubted any captive ever thought otherwise.

"Lily?" She looked up and realized both men were staring at her.

"What, Jed?"

"I just wanted to know how you felt. You looked lost in thought."

A weak smile pulled on her lips. "I was lost in thought. I'll be fine. I'm tougher than I look."

Smitty laughed. "I know darlin', I know."

———

JED ASKED AROUND but no one admitted to seeing anything. He did notice a few things though. A couple, Edward and Joanne Lanster were trying hard to hide their accents. They spoke differently every time he talked with them. Jed didn't know what accent they were hiding. They also had a young daughter named Izzy with them. He didn't know much about them. They followed all the rules and never gave him an ounce of trouble. They also kept to themselves. There was also a group of boys hanging about that hadn't been friends until recently. Quite likely they had thrown the rock, but he didn't have proof. Most people were indifferent, and he was frustrated.

Lily sat by their wagon. Their wagon. He liked the sound of it. But she probably wouldn't want a relationship with a man. He often wondered what she'd been through but he wasn't going to ask. It was her business.

"Are you alright?" he asked as he sat next to her.

"I have coffee, help yourself." She gave him a slight smile.

Jed poured himself a cup and topped off the coffee in her cup. "You didn't answer my question. Are you alright?"

"My head throbs a bit, but it's nothing. Looks like a party is going to happen."

He hated the longing in her voice. There was going to be a celebration for reaching Independence Rock, and he wished he could escort her. It would be heaven to have her in his arms as they danced.

"They'll start playing music any minute. A few of the other wagon trains will be celebrating too, so I expect it'll get pretty loud."

"I remember wanting to dance with you before…"

"I remember. I had to keep telling myself you were too young."

She nodded and sighed. "It seems like so long ago. It's funny how time can go so fast, and at other times, it goes so very slow. My last two years were very slow. Now I'm taking things moment by moment. Times like this with you go by quickly, but the times when I'm stared at and treated worse than mud on their shoes, goes slow. But I can't go back and change anything, and I'm finding it hard to regain my old life. I don't belong in either world. Every night I would think of what it would be like to be rescued. I thought people would be happy to see me. I never thought that they'd turn their backs on me for not killing myself. It took everything I had to survive. It would have been easy to die. Sometimes I'm not sure I made the right decision. But then there are moments like this where I can talk to you and I'm glad I'm back."

The first strains of music played and Jed stood and offered her his hand. She shyly put her hand in his and stood. He led her away from the fire, drew her into his arms, and led them in a dance. "You remember."

"I practiced a lot when I was young. I wanted to be the belle of the ball someday." A sigh slipped free. "I was foolish."

He pulled her closer. "Never foolish. I'm very glad you are here. I was going crazy with worry about you. It was almost as though without you the sun was never as bright as it once was. Never as bright as when you were here. I feel incredibly lucky to have found you."

He twirled her around the grass and they laughed and smiled. Finally they stopped but their gaze held. He leaned down and she tilted her head up toward him. Her lips looked so dewy soft as they slightly parted. He was tempted, so very tempted to kiss her but he couldn't. He kissed her forehead and took a step back.

"Thank you for the dance, Lily." He still held her hand as he walked them back to their fire. The silence between them grew and it was on the verge of uncomfortable.

"I'm going to try to sleep," she said as she slipped her hand from his. "Thank you. I had a fine time."

Before he had a chance to reply, she was in the wagon. And she had taken some of his happiness with her.

Jed walked around the circle of wagons making sure everything was going well. Sometimes things didn't go so well with other trains. He once saw feuding families on different trains try to kill each other. He spotted Ricky Richards watching Lily's wagon.

He snuck up on him. "What are you doing?"

The startled boy yelped. "I was just makin' sure Lily was fine. I heard Garber and Miss Wanda talkin' about how she could be kidnapped again and put on another train. I like Lily, and I'm makin' it my business to see that they don't steal her."

Jed nodded. "Good man. Next time come tell me so I don't shoot you by mistake."

"Yes, sir. I will!"

"I think I can take over for now. I'll let you know if I need you."

Ricky nodded and took off. He was a responsible young man.

Jed contemplated confronting Garber and Wanda but he decided not to tip them off. They'd just deny it. Lily had tried to stay out of their way but they just couldn't let it go. Why couldn't people just mind their own business?

"So far it's been fairly quiet," Rex said as he stood next to Jed. "It's strange but there haven't been many fights to break up. I think maybe it's because the group next to ours are all part of some religion. They don't dance but many of the men are good storytellers. It's been entertaining."

"I got a tip from Ricky Richardson. Garber and Wanda were talking about kidnapping Lily and giving her to one of the other trains." Jed ran his hand over his face. "I don't remember ever seeing them talking before."

"You sure Ricky is on the up and up? That boy is sweet on Lily."

"Seemed credible to me. He was standing guard right here when I found him."

Rex shook his head. "Come to think of it, they *were* talking for a bit. I thought maybe a romance was in the making. Other than that, Wanda has been with the women having a hen party."

Jed grinned.

"What's so funny?" Rex asked.

"I wonder what they'd do if they heard you call their gossip parties hen parties?"

"They don't take kindly to their discussions being called gossip parties either," Smitty whispered behind them. "If you two are on lookout, you aren't very good at it. You didn't even hear me coming up on ya."

"We heard you. Didn't we Rex? I know you pride yourself on being a silent walker, so I didn't let on."

Smitty laughed. "You keep telling yourself those fibs, but it's the kind of thing that can get you killed." He turned and walked in the other direction.

Rex shrugged his shoulders. "I didn't hear him, Jed."

Jed's lip twitched. "Neither did I. I'll stay here, you keep an eye out."

"Got it boss."

Jed leaned against a wagon wheel. Did Garber have a death wish? Maybe he was the one who'd tried to stab Lily through the wagon canvas. It was impossible to know for sure. Of course, Lily was changed from her time away, but she always watched how others did things in a public setting. She had nice manners and didn't eat with her hands like most people expected her to. She went along with everything that polite society expected. She was leaner and well-muscled. When he touched her, she didn't have an ounce of fat on her. Once in awhile, her English was halting but it was getting much better. The only thing was the color of her skin. You could tell she'd spent much time outside without a bonnet on. Why should it make much of a difference?

All was right in camp. Couples walked hand in hand and children ran. It was a good feeling to be at Independence Rock before Independence Day. It meant they were ahead of schedule. He had no way of knowing what was ahead that might slow them down.

The celebration was winding down, and he kept watch from the shadows of a nearby wagon's wheel. Garber and Wanda strolled by hand in hand. They stopped for a moment and looked around. Then they whispered for a moment and looked around again. Garber shook his head but Wanda kept pulling at his sleeve. Garber reached down into his boot and drew out a long bladed knife.

"Evening, Wanda, Garber. Nice night don't you think?" Jed had his gun drawn but he still leaned against the wagon wheel.

Garber turned pale while Wanda's face flushed deep red.

"Jed, didn't see you there," Garber said in a lazy trying-to–sound-innocent voice. He leaned down and returned his knife to his boot.

"I've been watching you most of the evening," Jed lied.

Garber and Wanda exchanged flustered gazes.

"Garber has asked me to marry him," Wanda tried to smile.

Jed wasn't buying it. "What did your brother have to say? He gave you his blessing didn't he? You know, we can have the reverend perform the wedding tomorrow. Won't that be a fine thing?" Jed had to bit his lip to keep from laughing at Garber's expression a deep dismay.

Wanda swallowed hard. "We're off to find my brother now. Promise me you won't tell anyone until I tell him."

"Well if you're going to tell Dave now, I won't have to keep the secret long. Congratulations."

"Well, err, thanks," Garber mumbled. "Let's get going, Wanda."

Jed watched as they walked away. They seemed to be arguing about something. He couldn't help the big grin that spread. It would serve them right to be stuck with each other. His smile faded. They were a real threat to Lily. Garber had his knife out, and Jed was fairly certain the man had planned to use it.

He'd make sure that Garber's wagon was nowhere near Wanda's. This way he could see if they crossed the wagon circle to see one another. He'd alert the others on guard to let him know if they meet. Unless they did get married. He shook his head. They were idiots but dangerous ones.

CHAPTER FIVE

*L*ily drove the wagon with her gun at her side and her knife strapped to her leg. It had been three weeks since they'd left Independence Rock, and the hair on the back of her neck was constantly standing on end. At first, she thought it to be Garber and Wanda but they really didn't scare her. She just had a bad feeling and she planned to be ready.

They were getting ready to ford the Sweetwater River for the third time. Jed said they'd end up fording it six times before they were done. The water didn't scare her, but the tension within the party was always high. So far, the crossings had been uneventful but they'd been warned that the water for the next one was higher than usual.

The closer they got, the louder the rushing water sounded. It was extremely fast moving, with dangerous looking white rapids. Surely there was a better place to cross. She scanned up and down the river and sighed; no place looked safe.

Smitty always went first. Then he immediately built a fire on the bank in case anyone ended up in the water. Rex rode downriver and waited in case he needed to pluck anyone out of the water. It had been the same at each crossing, but she knew this one was not the same.

She held her breath when Smitty crossed. He made it look easy. Perhaps she needed to relax a bit. The line moved slowly, and it was finally her turn. With a stiff grip on the traces, she drove the oxen into the river. The roaring of the water was louder than anything else she'd heard in awhile. It was a great relief when she made it to the next bank.

Behind her were the Scotts. Tara sat on the front bench with her father. Lily heard a scream and instantly pulled the brake and tied off the reins. She jumped down and saw Tara bobbing up and down in the fast-moving water.

Jed quickly crossed and rode along the bank. Then there was a gunshot. Lily couldn't see what was going on, so she began to run. She'd become a rather swift runner the last two years and she was the first to reach the Indian lying on the ground. She gasped as she recognized Chayton, the Sioux warrior that had kidnapped her. Blood pooled under him. Eyes wide, she looked around for Jed; he must have shot Chayton.

Dropping to her knees, she checked the Sioux's wound. It was a death wound, and they both knew it.

"*Chumani*, my heart. They stole you away from me," Chayton said. He winced as he tried to move.

"Chayton, you are on a fool's errand. I am with my people now. I want to be with my people." Lily put his head in her lap. "You should have stayed with the tribe."

His black eyes flashed in anger. "I came after my woman. You belong to me. They had no right to sell you while I was on a hunt."

Lily brushed her hand along his cheekbone. "I belong to no one. I was never your woman, and you know that. I do thank you for your many kindnesses, but in my heart I can't forgive that you stole me from my mother. She is now dead."

"If I had the chance to do it over, I would still take you with me. You are so beautiful." He coughed a few times. "*Techihhila*." His body went limp.

Sensing she wasn't alone she glanced up. "He's dead," she said to Jed. She gently lay Chayton's head on the ground and stood. "How did Tara fare?"

"She's mad as a wet hen but she'll be fine. She has some cuts and bruises from the rocks on the water. An arrow hit one of their oxen."

"Is the ox dead?"

"No, just mad. Let's get you back." He took her hand then stopped. "You knew him."

She nodded. "Yes, Chayton was the one who stole me that day in the river. He came to take me again."

"He's far from home, isn't he?"

"Yes, and it appears he traveled alone. I was traded to the trappers when he was away from the village. It made him angry." She sighed. Her body began to shake.

Jed took her into his arms and held her, but she didn't find comfort. She'd hated Chayton but felt no relief at his death. Tara had almost drowned, and it was her fault. The death would have been on her head.

"You don't have to worry about him anymore. You were mighty brave running through the woods. It was a sight to behold."

She tilted her head until she caught his gaze. "I thought it was you who was hurt. I came as fast as I could to help you. I caught a glimpse of the arrow and then heard the shot. His arrow landed true. He probably planned to distract everyone so he could take me."

"He must have cared for you."

She stepped out of his arms and turned her back on him.

"No, it wasn't about caring or love. It was about his pride. He owned me, and to him I was stolen away."

"If you don't mind me asking, what did he say to you?" Jed's voice was so soft and gentle. It was such a contrast to how Chayton used to yell at her.

"He said I was beautiful and that he loved me." She sighed. "We'd best get back. They'll want to string me up again."

"I'm sure it's nothing that drastic." Jed didn't sound very confident.

Turning back toward him, she gave him a nod. "Let's go." They walked quickly and silently. *Techihhila?* How could Chayton say he loved her when he treated her like a dog? He'd never so much as favored her with a smile. No, there was no love between them. He was an abusive prideful man who didn't have love in him to give. His tribe would mourn him when he didn't return, and Lily was sad for his mother, Macawi. Her lips twitched.

"What is it?" Jed asked.

"I was just thinking about his mother. Her name is Macawi, which means generous. The funny thing is that she was the stingiest woman on earth. She was the type that wouldn't give a bare bone to a dying dog."

"You knew her well."

"I was her slave. Chayton owned me but I was her slave. I knew her too well. She'd rather hit and kick than try to teach me to speak her language. Chayton taught me a bit at a time. Let's not speak of it now. I'm trying to forget all that."

Jed smiled at her. "Yes, it sounds best forgotten. I'm sure we have a bunch of questions to answer at camp."

Her body chilled, and she wished she could just walk away from it all. Everyone except for Jed, Smitty,Owen and Rex.

JED'S STOMACH tightened at the angry faces he viewed back at camp. Tara was still crying, wailing was more accurate. She was now wearing dry clothes and drinking what looked to be a bit of whiskey at Smitty's fire.

The rest of the party watched as he and Lily approached.

Tara's father took a step forward. "How dare you bring that, that Indian back here? She's the reason my poor Tara almost drowned. I want her gone, banished, killed. I don't care what but I won't have her near my family!" His face grew redder as he talked.

"How is Tara?" Jed asked.

"She's beyond upset. We all are!" her father yelled.

Jed nodded, took Lily's hand, and walked to the fire. "You can get in the wagon if you like," he whispered to her.

"No," she replied as she lifted her head and stared out at the crowd.

"The Indian who shot the arrow is dead—"

"You should have scalped him!" A man in the crowd shouted.

"There was no sign of any other Indians in the area so we think he acted alone," Jed continued. "The best thing for us to do is to get in our wagons and put some distance between us and the dead Indian."

Wanda pointed her finger at Lily. "This is her fault! She led that Indian here. Tara could have been killed. And why is her dress so bloody?"

Lily opened her mouth but Jed talked faster. "I shot the Indian but he wasn't dead. He was about to shoot an arrow at me when Lily threw her knife at him, killing him. She went to see if he was dead or if she could save him. That's why she has blood on her." Lily's eyes widened at his lies.

"Still it's a lot of blood," Wanda said with a sniff.

"I held his head in my lap as he died. It was the least I could do," Lily explained.

Jed held up his hand to silence the protests from the crowd. "Listen folks, we're moving on. Be ready in a quarter hour." He stood until the crowd dispersed. A chill went up his spine. This wasn't the end of it, and he had a feeling it was going to get a lot worse before it got better.

He took the mug of coffee Smitty offered. "How's the ox? Did you have to put him down?"

Smitty shook his head. "The arrow went through his ear. Good shot that Indian had. Listen, I hate to tell you this, but things were getting pretty tense around here."

"Let me guess, they want to lynch her."

Smitty nodded. "That about sums it up. I want her riding with me today. One of the other boys can drive your wagon. I don't trust anyone now. Most are out for blood."

"There's been enough bloodshed. I'll take Lily to our wagon so she can get changed, then she'll ride with you."

Smitty nodded. "That was some whopper you told the group. You killed that Indian, not her."

"Smitty, think what you want. You always seem to know the truth of things."

Smitty smiled. "When it comes to you and your brothers, I could always ferret what was really going on."

Jed smiled back. "Lily, let's go and get you washed up."

A WHILE later Jed yelled "Wagons ho!" It was a relief to be moving again. He was more than a little afraid for Lily. People refused to listen to reason. They all believed that Lily had invited the Indian and that Tara ending up in the river was Lily's fault as well. He felt bad for Tara's scary incident and wished he could have prevented it, but neither he nor Lily had any way to know what was about to happen.

"Everything all right?" Rex asked as he rode alongside Jed.

"Heck, nothing seems right. What was the reverend doing

while we were in the woods? Was he trying to calm people down? Was he giving Tara some sympathy?"

"I hate to say it, but he was in his wagon with his sister. I've never been one to say anything bad about a preacher but this one is never there when there's trouble. I'm beginning to wonder if he even has a Bible. Did you notice he doesn't hold one during funerals? Strange if you ask me."

"That's what I like about you, Rex. You're very observant. Keep an eye out for Lily and Smitty. I have a bad feeling."

Rex took off his hat and wiped his brow with his sleeve. "You got it, boss." He turned his bay horse and rode down the line of wagons.

The rest of the day was uneventful. Jed did notice that Lily held a rifle across her lap. It was probably a good idea. He just wasn't sure how to handle the disgruntled group. They wanted Lily gone, and that wasn't happening. He just wasn't sure how to keep her safe. He couldn't leave the train; he had an obligation to the party.

He'd drive them a bit longer than usual. Perhaps they'd be too tired to fight much.

THE WHEELS SLOWED as the sun began to lower in the sky. The sky had a peaceful pink and purple color to it, but Lily knew the calm to be a charade. She'd be lucky if she didn't get her throat slashed by the end of the night. She could feel the tension even driving with Smitty, the tension could be felt.

Why had Jed lied to them by telling them she threw a knife at Chayton? She hated lies. It had halted the crowd for barely a minute. Her stomach had lurched when that man called for a scalp. It always made her queasy to see scalps hanging from lances and belts. No matter where a person stood, there were good and bad people on either side. Right now it was the white people she was afraid of.

She offered to unyoke and unharness the oxen, but Smitty wouldn't hear of it. So instead, she grabbed wood and started the fire. They were going to need more wood. Most of the easily found branches had already been picked up, probably by other wagon trains. She walked deeper into the forest. She had to pull dead branches down off trees but it wasn't anything she hadn't done a million times before.

The back of her neck prickled. Someone was watching her again. Leaning down she grabbed her knife and kept it in her hand. Instead of carrying the wood bundle from tree to tree she left it and brought wood back to it. She stopped often and listened and it didn't take long before she saw Garber. He hadn't yet seen her.

"Looking for wood too?" she asked as she raised her right brow.

At first, he seemed startled, then his face contorted in rage. "I was looking for you. Looks like I found you."

She kept a safe difference between them. "I'm here, so say what you have to say and get going."

A sick grin crossed his face. "I wasn't planning on talking. My original intent was to have me some fun with you. I know you were giving it away for free to those young bucks. Then I thought choking you would be the perfect topper."

"I thought you and Wanda were engaged. It wouldn't be right to try for me when you have an intended."

He shook his head. "How stupid do you think I am? I'd never marry that harpy. I've had my eye on you since the beginning. I don't think one more man would matter."

She gradually backed a few steps away from him. "I'm sorry to disappoint you but the gossips have been working overtime. I can go to my future husband intact and with a clear conscience."

Garber laughed. "Everyone knows that Indians rape white women. You don't have to lie. It's going to happen either way."

She felt like a cat ready to spring as she gripped her knife ready to defend herself. Adrenaline coursed through her body.

"I found her!" Owen shouted as he stepped into view. "Is there a problem here?" He glared at Garber.

Rage filled Garber's eyes as he pressed his lips into a grim, straight line. "No, just gathering some wood is all." He quickly looked around. "Who are you shouting to?"

Rex appeared, gun in hand. "That would be me. We're gathering wood too. I suggest we all go back to camp. And Garber? Stay away from Lily."

They didn't wait for an answer as Lily walked away from Garber flanked by her two escorts. She led them to the pile of wood she'd gathered. "No sense in leaving it here. Not when I have such strong men to carry it."

Owen grunted as he picked up the whole pile. "I don't think Jed would think wood is worth your safety. You do know that Garber planned to harm you?"

"No more wandering away from camp, Lily. Jed was mad when he couldn't find you, and I have to say, Jed isn't much fun when he's angry."

"I'm sorry you had to come looking for me." The knot in her stomach tightened as camp came into view. Jed paced in front of Smitty's wagon with his hands clenched.

He turned as they came out of the woods. His expression changed from fury to concern. "Where were you?"

"Getting more wood. I know it sounds like a poor excuse, but I needed to get away from all the prying eyes. It was too much." She sat down and added wood to the fire. "I'm sorry I worried you."

Owen stepped forward. "It's a good thing you sent us. Garber was threatening her."

Jed swallowed hard. "What happened?" He stared at her.

"He planned to rape then kill me. I had my knife so it wouldn't have happened. I just didn't want to be blamed for his death. He is a coward and is too fat to move quick enough. I am grateful you sent Owen and Rex to find me. Now I don't have blood on my hands."

"Lily—"

"I have to help make some food for us. We can discuss it later. Please don't go after Garber. It'll be his word against mine, and we all know my word is worthless."

Jed nodded. "I'll leave it be for the moment, but I'm not making any promises for the future."

"Fair enough." She set the beans that had been soaking all day over the fire and then cut up fatback and onion. She added all ingredients together and gave the pot a stir. "How about hoecakes instead of biscuits?" She tried to sound as normal as possible. How the situation with Garber would play out was anyone's guess but somehow it would be to her detriment.

Finally, the men left her to her cooking. She'd forgotten just how complicated the white man's world was. There was always someone who wasn't happy. She mixed the batter for the hoecakes when a shadow blocked the setting sun. It was a surprise to see Tara. Lily had a feeling she should feel dismay.

"Lily, I just wanted you to know how grateful I am that you saved Jed. He's a good man with an incredible future. I just hate all this talk about you and how it reflects poorly on Jed. People are beginning to question his leadership skills."

"I don't think it's his leadership they question. It's me they don't like." Lily put her hands on her hips and calmly stared at Tara.

"Well, yes that is the real problem. I was thinking we

could leave you at the next fort. You must have someone out there missing you. It would be the best thing you could do for Jed. It sounds like he has a great ranch with his brothers, and they are well known in the community. I'd hate for him to have a mark against him for his behavior on this train."

Lily furrowed her brow. "His behavior? I don't understand what you are saying. He has been a great leader and has used all his skills to keep us safe."

Tara gave her a condescending smile. "You've been away from regular people too long. Skills don't matter as much as a reputation. Right now, his reputation as an upright, moral, strong leader is in question and it's because of his association with you. I know it's hard to hear but it's true. I'm not trying to hurt you."

There was a lot of merit in what she said, and Lily's heart dropped. She hadn't thought about how people looked at Jed now. She was taunting him with her presence. "I understand. Thank you for telling me, and I'm glad you weren't harmed."

Tara smiled and nodded. "I'll let you get back to what you were doing. I'm glad we had this little talk."

Tara's hips swayed back and forth as she walked away. It must be nice to be Tara. People liked her and accepted her. She'd be a good wife to someone… Her heart squeezed. Tara would be a good wife for Jed. They'd have beautiful children. Washington Territory was sounding better and better. She'd bet she could find a guide at the next fort. Jed said she had money in a bank somewhere. She'd be able to make a life out there. It was probably for the best if she was alone.

She had no claim on Jed. He was just a friend, and friends did what was best for one another. She'd have to find out what fort they were stopping at next. It was time to let go.

CHAPTER SIX

The last few weeks had been tense and frustrating for Lily. They were almost to the Continental Divide, and they had been escorted by several Indians. She wasn't sure what tribe they were from, but they mainly wanted to trade. The groups seemed to go from train to train but since all Indians looked alike to the *Wasichu*, the white people, everyone on the train thought the same group was following them the whole time.

Many were vocal about Lily having to leave. She drove the wagon during the day and stayed in it more than she wanted when they stopped. Jed still slept under her wagon at night. Fort Bridger was the next fort, and there had been a call to leave her there. Of course Jed told them no, but she was thinking it might be for the best.

He had a great reputation as a guide, and she couldn't take that from him. She'd be safe at the fort until she decided on a plan. Maybe she could hire someone to take her to the Pacific Northwest. It sounded idyllic to her. She'd build a shelter and there would be no problem surviving. She knew all there was to know about hunting and preserving meat.

She knew how to make furs to keep her warm and how to keep herself healthy.

She'd need some supplies to start including a rifle. Hopefully she could get all that at the fort. She heard Jed announce they were going across the divide and had reached the South pass. Three more miles and they would be at the Pacific Springs. They'd spend a few days there.

Many shouted *yahoo* but she wasn't exactly certain why. They hadn't made it to a fort yet and they certainly hadn't made it to Oregon. Taking a few days to rest wasn't what she wanted. She'd made her decision to leave and she didn't want to dwell on it. Every glance, every touch ignited her. How was she going to be able to say goodbye to Jed? The thought of being so apart from him again broke her heart but it was the right thing to do.

They'd been slowly ascending all these weeks and she expected to be going back down the mountain but to her surprise, there was rolling prairie all around. It didn't take long until they stopped. The women would all bathe she supposed. A shudder went through her. Her experience of being taken while bathing in the river still paralyzed her.

She kept herself cleaner than anyone just so they couldn't call her a dirty Indian. She made sure she had the best manners, and she tried to smile at people. But no matter, people still wanted her gone. Garber and Wanda still put their noses in the air as they walked by, still hand in hand. Then there was Tara who tried everything to be alone with Jed. It was amusing to watch Jed get out of situations.

Ricky Richards didn't care how much trouble he got in with his father. He refused to stop guarding her. Of course, he thought she didn't know. Quite the cast of characters. Jill Callen smiled at her but her reverend brother often glared at her. They didn't bother her. The most interesting family was the Landsters. Edward, Joanne, and Izzy all try to cover their

British accents. It was almost comical to see their expressions when one of them forgot. Lily figured they were running from something.

The wagons slowed and began to circle. She sighed. Should she hide in the wagon again or go and help Smitty? It was tempting to hide, but she'd stayed inside long enough.

"Everything all right?" Rex asked as he stopped his horse near her.

"Sure. How much longer until we get to Oregon?"

"We just passed the halfway mark. We're making good time." Rex touched the brim of his hat before he rode on.

Halfway? Oh dear, how was she to survive? That clinched it. She was going to find a guide to take her to Washington Territory. How far away was it? She frowned as she walked to Smitty's wagon.

"Hey, Smitty how far is it to Washington?" She automatically began to make biscuits.

"Farther than Oregon. I've never been there so I don't rightly know, but I would think it would be at least another month of travel. There aren't many great trails for wagons. There are a lot of prospectors who go that way."

"Prospectors?"

Smitty nodded. "Gold miners. But who's to say there's even gold up there? It's an untamed land." He cut up some fresh venison. "Wait, you're not planning to go there are you?"

She nodded.

"Last I heard you were coming back to the ranch with us. What happened?"

She glanced away. She couldn't look at him. "I just think it would be best."

He groaned. "It's your business but you need to tell Jed. You can't spring it on him after the journey. It wouldn't be right."

"Tell me what?"

Her head turned when she heard Jed. "Oh, nothing really. I'm going to go and live up in the northwest. I think I would be more suited to life there."

He stared at her as though he'd never seen her before. "I know you asked me once what it was like there but I had no idea you planned to live up there." His Adam's apple bobbed up and down. "I have guard duty. I'll be late." He strode off.

"Well, you gone and done it," Smitty said. "You broke that man's heart." He shook his head.

"He doesn't think of me that way." She bit her bottom lip. Was she so wrong?

"I don't know how you missed it but that young man is all tangled up in you. You didn't know that?"

She wiped her floured hands on her apron and sat down. "He never said, I mean I don't see him all that much lately. I figured he'd be just as happy if I left."

Smitty sat down next to her. "Look and listen with your heart. I think it's a skill you've forgotten. Jed is known for wearing his heart on his sleeve. You're the woman he wants."

She furrowed her brow. Could it be true? "He's been very kind to me."

Smitty nodded. "Like I said, look and listen with your heart, and I think you'll see clearly how he feels."

They cooked together in comfortable silence. As much as she wanted to believe, she just couldn't. Maybe her heart wasn't working that way anymore. Perhaps her time with the Sioux stopped her from completely trusting in anyone. But she would take Smitty's advice.

JED SEETHED AS he guarded the women bathing. Of course he had his back to them but the more he listened to them the uglier he found them to be, and it wasn't something he wanted to know. What was wrong with these women? Didn't they know he was there? If he heard the words "dirty Indian" again he was going to snap.

They claimed to be good God-fearing folks, but they could do with some lessons in Christian charity. And now Lily didn't want to come home with him. The women on the ranch would welcome her with open arms, but maybe he hadn't explained it so well for her.

Did she really want to live alone? Maybe she just didn't want to be around him. His heart squeezed thinking about letting her go her own way. She was very independent, and she didn't need a man around. Did she ever think about marriage and children?

His jaw dropped. Where had those thoughts come from? He didn't have plans for a wife and kids. No, he was foot-loose and fancy free. There was no ball and chain shackled to his leg. He'd never be henpecked.

"You're not peeking are you?" Tara asked. A lot of laughter erupted.

He waited for it to die down. "No, not my style. I'm sure you ladies are about done? I've been standing here a good while."

There was a bit of grumbling, but he heard the sound of them getting out of the water and the swish of cloth told him they were getting dressed. He counted heads as they went by, and one was missing.

"Hurry up!"

"Why don't you come and help me?" Tara asked coyly.

"Can't. Just get dressed."

"Why not? No one would know."

Jed shook his head. "I would know. I don't lower my morals or standards just because no one would know. I would know. Now get dressed!"

"Well, that's good to know. For a time I thought that maybe you and Lily had something going on, but you wouldn't lower yourself that low." She bounced on her way to the camp with a happy smile on her face.

Jed pushed off from the tree he leaned against, and his stomach dropped when he saw the hurt on Lily's face. "I'll stand guard if you—"

"No I came to fill my buckets and get them heated. If Tara wants to be your woman, why don't you want her?"

Some of the tension went out of his body. "I don't happen to like her very much. She can be mean spirited."

Lily filled one bucket and then another. She stood and gazed at him as though he was a puzzle she was trying to figure out. "She's very pretty, and the other travelers all like her."

"I don't give a fig what others think. I've seen a lot in the years I've been guiding wagon trains. I don't know, I thought most people had good hearts but it's simply not true. Everyone has their own agenda and not everyone is willing to help those in need. I've made plenty of friends though, too, lifelong friends. Of course, I have my brothers and Smitty. All I know is that I will not live my life with a person I don't care for." He took the buckets from her. "Let's get the water heated for you. I'll put up a makeshift privacy curtain for you."

She rewarded him with a smile. "You're too good to me. You must realize being my friend isn't earning you any points with the rest of the people."

He smiled back. "Like I said, I don't give a fig." He built up her fire and put the buckets close to warm. Next, he grabbed a washtub, a rope, and a blanket and created some privacy for her.

Standing outside the blanket guarding Lily was turning into agony for Jed. The pictures of what Lily looked like bathing wouldn't go away. He tried counting, he tried to remember jokes he'd heard, he tried thinking of her as a sister. Dang, he kept thinking about how soft her skin was and how nice it would be to touch it.

He shifted from one foot to the other and inwardly groaned. "Almost done?" He heard the sound of the water splashing as she got out. He was relieved, but his mind wouldn't stop. He was like a lovesick schoolboy, and that didn't make him happy.

"I'm finished getting dressed." She came out from behind the blanket in her nightdress and a shawl wrapped around her. "Thank you so much—"

Jed cupped her face with his palms and kissed her soundly. Then he jumped back. He was stepping into fire, and he had to get out of there. "I'll empty the water. Good night." He could feel her gaze on him as he turned away. He needed to get ahold of himself.

DAYS OF REST were good for the oxen, but they weren't as good for Lily. Being idle was driving her crazy. She'd done all her chores within the first hours of their first full day at Pacific Springs. She even offered to repair any torn clothing Smitty and the men had, but apparently Rex had been spending time with a widow who was magical with a needle.

The whole day she felt both Garber and Wanda's heated gaze upon her. Why their hate was so great, she had no idea. She wanted to be the girl she was for just a bit of time. The girl who didn't know of the cruelties of people. Back when all she wanted was for Jed to smile at her. She sighed. Those days were well over.

She watched as Tara threw herself in Jed's path at every turn. Most of the time he looked annoyed and Lily wanted to bubble up with laughter but she just watched with her features expressionless.

Winston Richards passed by her fire a few times before he stopped. Lily didn't stand, just remained seated on her crate. The polite thing to do would be to offer coffee, but she wasn't feeling polite.

He tipped his hat to her. He appeared so much bigger and wider since she was sitting. "I would like to talk to you about something."

She raised her brow. "Talk or tell?"

A frown took over his beefy face. "What do you mean?"

"What I mean is, are you here to talk to me about your son or to tell me to stay away from him? But since there is no reason to tell, let me do the talking. I have no interest in your son. I already know how you feel about me, and I would not go against a boy's father. You see that's what he is; he's still a boy. I hope it's nothing more than curiosity, and I certainly have not encouraged him in any way."

Winston swallowed hard. "I appreciate it ma'am. He is just a boy who doesn't know his own mind. Good day." He tapped the brim of his hat before he left.

That boy should not have so much time with nothing to do. He needed to learn skills to survive, but she wasn't his parent.

Would she feel lonely if she went to Washington? Was being by yourself better than feeling alone with people around? She pondered for a while and decided that being totally alone was preferable. What was Jed's ranch like? Smitty seemed to think it a wonderful place. She was so lost in thought, she didn't hear anyone behind her until she felt the knife go into her back.

She yelped and tried to reach to get it out. Stretching her right arm over her shoulder, she couldn't even touch the hilt. When she lifted her left arm, searing pain tore through her.

Moaning, she twisted and turned, but the knife remained out of her reach. Blood poured down her back and dripped onto the ground at her feet. She was focused on removing it she didn't see who did it. Blast it! She heard a scream and saw Jill staring at her and pointing. Lily started to sway and would have ended up in the fire face down if Jed hadn't caught her.

He pulled out the knife and let it drop to the ground. She wanted to tell him to grab it so they could see who it belonged to but she seemed to be beyond speech.

"Put her in my wagon," Smitty instructed.

Jed carried her, and Smitty climbed in before them so they could position her on her stomach. She heard the tearing of her dress and bemoaned the loss of it. Who? Who was it? She cried out. Smitty was cleaning her wound with something she wished was never known to man.

"It's deep, and I'll need to stitch you up. It's going to hurt but you were lucky. If they were aiming for your heart, they missed," Smitty said as he pulled a needle and thread out of his medicine box.

"Jed?" She hoped he could hear her. Her throat felt odd.

"I'm here, honey."

"Find the knife. Find the knife," she croaked out.

She was thankful Smitty put a piece of wood between her teeth before he began stitching. That way her screams wouldn't be heard throughout the camp. It was far better than being cauterized, but it still hurt beyond bearing. How stupid could she be? She knew better than to allow anyone to sneak up on her. She'd let her guard down, and that was unacceptable. Death could have been her fate.

It was stupid for the assassin to miss her heart. It couldn't have been a seasoned hunter. She'd been sitting still. It made no sense. There was a camp full of suspects, but she couldn't reason out who it could have been, and she doubted she'd be allowed to examine the footprints.

"All done. Now that wasn't so bad was it?" She heard the humor in Smitty's words but she didn't smile.

She took out the piece of wood and sighed in relief. The worst part was over. The wagon rocked as Smitty got out, and then it rocked again as Jed climbed in.

"The knife was gone. I'm sorry. I should have been there." She could hear the defeat underlying his anger. "I should have at least assigned someone to watch you."

It was hard to look at Jed while lying on her stomach. "Don't blame yourself. I can usually defend myself, but I wasn't paying attention. I can't figure out who did it. Did you look for footprints? Were they big or small?"

"Honey, the whole place had been trampled by the time I got back there. I did ask, but no one knew about the knife."

She'd have to find out on her own but if it was the last thing she ever did, she'd ferret out the stabber.

"We could stay a few more days here if you'd like—"

Alarm ran through her. "No! I mean I don't need extra time. I can probably drive the wagon tomorrow."

Jed laughed. "No driving but we'll continue on. I won't feel at ease until I have you settled on my ranch." He kissed her cheek. "I'll be sleeping under you tonight. Funny to think we'll be facing each other but with a floor between us."

"Real funny. Jed? Thank you for everything."

"Anytime, honey."

CHAPTER SEVEN

Two days later, they were almost to Fort Bridger and Lily was on pins and needles wondering if she should leave the wagon train. It would probably be doing everyone a favor if she left. She sat on the wagon bench while Rex drove. Everywhere she looked there were Indians trying to sell items they'd made. Rex told her that many were trappers' wives.

Pondering what the other travelers probably thought, she cringed. She wondered what it was like for these women to be wives of white men. They probably felt out of place as much as she did. She was sorry for them. Had they been sold to the trappers? She didn't have to use her imagination about the looks of disdain they were getting from her group. She'd seen all the glares before.

"How many soldiers will be at the fort, do you think?" she asked Rex.

He cocked his brow at her. "There's no soldiers there, just some supplies."

She frowned. "I thought a fort was a place where soldiers were garrisoned. How can it be a fort then?"

"Mr. Briggs owns it and he named it Fort Briggs, I suppose. I think we have plenty of supplies, but there are some in our group that aren't as blessed. There isn't a big selection, and the prices are high."

Nodding, she turned and looked at the scenery. She didn't have a decision to make, not yet anyway. She wouldn't be safe in such a place without soldiers. Out of sorts was how'd she describe it. Jed expected her to live on his ranch. The group wanted her gone. One wanted her dead. Smitty was under the wrong impression that Jed cared for her. It was hard to make sense of it all.

Would she have been able to leave if Fort Briggs was a real fort? She wasn't sure. She longed for Jed at times but she reeled her feelings back every time. He was too good for her. He might not think that but he'd regret any relationship they had. His friends in Oregon wouldn't approve. Heaven help her but she wouldn't be able to resist him if he kissed her again.

Her cheeks burned as they traveled on. Her mother and her counsel was deeply missed. She was so deep in thought she didn't notice they had stopped.

"Don't you dare try to climb down yourself!" Jed yelled as he made a beeline for her.

She swallowed hard. Her decision had just been made for her. She loved him and she'd have to leave him. She cherished the moment she was held in his arms as he lifted her down. He smiled at her and she smiled back but her heart broke for what could have been. "Thank you."

"Always a pleasure. Would you like me to escort you to the store?" He looked so happy and she didn't want to break the spell.

"That would be lovely. Thank you." She put her arm through his and was warmed when he covered her hand with his. He smelled of leather and horses with a hint of cinnamon. He liked a bit of cinnamon in his coffee when he could get it. She'd never known anyone else to add it. As they walked, she was once again impressed how well he'd filled out. He was a tall, well-muscled man now. When she'd thought of him during her captivity, she always pictured him as the boy she had left. She'd allow herself a few nice hours with Jed and then she'd have to turn her heart off, if she could.

"We're in for a storm tonight," Jed said.

She glanced up. "There isn't a cloud in the sky."

He chuckled. "I'll bet you a kiss we get a storm tonight." His eyes had a mischievous sparkle.

She looked in all directions and smiled. "You're on. It's too bad but you won't be getting any kisses."

He gave her hand a light squeeze. "We'll see."

THREE HOURS LATER, Jed stuck his head into Lily's wagon. "Shall I collect now or do you want to wait until tomorrow evening. It's going to rain all day tomorrow." He laughed when her jaw dropped.

"I'll pay up later, thank you very much. I don't think you play fair, Jed Todd. I seem to remember you predicting weather on the first wagon train I was on."

"Then you should have known better." He winked at her and then went back into the pouring rain. He had a bad feeling someone was going to try to hurt her again tonight. She was right, he always knew when the bad weather was coming and for how long it would last. Uncanny really, just something that happened. He had to admit he'd won many bets with his predictions.

Gunshots tore through the silence but they didn't come from anyplace near Lily's wagon. They were on the other

85

side of the circle. The rain was coming down so hard he could hardly see in front of him. He did make out someone in a black duster with a rifle running away from the Landster wagon. Jed hurried as fast as he could and was shocked when he looked inside the wagon.

They all looked to be dead. One on top of another with the little girl Izzy on the bottom. There was so much blood, his stomach turned. A thin cry reached his ears, and he realized Izzy was still alive. He moved aside the bodies of her father and mother, and when he reached Izzy, her dress and hair were covered in blood.

Grabbing her, he lifted her out and handed her off to Owen. "Take her to Lily." After Owen was swallowed by the darkness, Jed yelled for the rest of the men. "Be on the lookout for a man in a black coat and carrying a rifle. I need a few of you to guard this wagon."

If it was a robbery gone bad, he sure as heck wanted to know what was in that wagon.

He kicked at the mud with enough force for it to splatter Smitty in the face. "Dang it! I'm sorry Smitty. Izzy is in Lily's wagon. Would you—"

Smitty already had his medicine box in his hands. "On my way!"

"Rex, come with me. We're going to Briggs' place to see if anyone there knows anything about this." He could hardly see Rex, but the other man fell into step beside him.

They went through the door with guns drawn, but the only ones in there were Briggs and his two workers. They were all dry.

After Jed explained what had happened to the Landsters, Briggs promised to let him know if he saw the man. Jed nodded and he and Rex braved the storm again.

Seeing no sign of the killer, they headed back to the Landster's wagon. It didn't make a lick of sense. Once the bodies were removed, Jed planned to come back and go through everything to look for clues.

"Be careful out here, Rex. I'm going to check on Izzy." Jed didn't wait for an answer. He just hustled off toward lily's wagon. A crowd had gathered. Most were holding on to their hats against the strong wind. Jed elbowed his way to the front and climbed into the wagon.

Izzy was lying peacefully in Lily's lap.

"Was she hit?"

Smitty shook his head. "She was spared all that. She's a bit out of her head. All she saw was the rifle as it poked through the back of the wagon. She did hear him check her parents afterward, and she closed her eyes pretending to be dead. The shooter didn't say anything, just grunted. I gave her something to sleep."

"That's for the best. Lily, is it hurting you to hold her that way?" Jed searched her expression for signs of discomfort.

"I'm fine."

She didn't look fine. "I'm going to put on some dry clothes so if you'd kindly close your eyes or look away. I'd appreciate it." He grinned at her but she just nodded and looked away.

It didn't take long, and soon he was sitting next to Lily. He gently took Izzy and placed her on his lap. "You need to rest too, Lily." He was rewarded with a grateful smile.

"Heck, I thought *I'd* be a target tonight. I was ready." She showed him a belt with a knife sheath she'd made from her deerskin dress. It was impressive.

"You planning to wear that around the camp?"

She nodded. "I want everyone to know I can defend myself if needed."

He nodded slowly. "What if it makes people more anxious about you?"

"I'm not going to let people scare me or put me in a

corner full of unwanted people. I really don't care if they like it or not. I need to be able to pull this knife as fast as lightning. I can't do that if I put the belt under my dress." Her eyes flashed with determination.

"I saw you that morning of the attack. You jumped out of the wagon and landed skillfully on your feet, crouching and looking for the enemy. It was very impressive. You learned a lot in the two years you were gone."

She sighed. "I wasn't gone. I was a prisoner. I have scars on my body from learning how to defend myself. Chayton was kind enough to trust me with a weapon. He did teach me. I think he was afraid for me as another woman wanted him for her husband. He never did understand I didn't want to marry."

"He didn't—"

"No! If he'd asked and I refused then maybe he would have. I saw it happen to other white women. The only intimacy we ever had was him combing my hair after I washed it and before he stained it with herbs. He liked the blondness. His mother was a force of her own and wouldn't have allowed him to touch me. She hated me at first. She'd hit me with a stick every few minutes it seemed. I had no idea what she was saying but she didn't care. I became quick at dodging her, and I think I won her respect. I worked hard."

Her eyes grew wet.

"You don't have to tell me." He tried to make his voice as soft as he could.

She shook her head and took a deep breath.

"Another captive always shrieked and cried. One night I heard the most awful screams and whimpers. She was gone the next day. I don't know what they did to her. I don't want to know." A shudder rolled through her. "I worked all the harder and I learned their language. I think I told you that Chayton taught me. It wasn't easy. There were times when we had no food, and the winters were horrendous, but I survived."

Jed nodded. "I'm glad you did. I kept hoping to hear word of you. I made friends with many trappers and traders. No one had seen you. People told me I was a fool to keep looking but I couldn't help it." He smiled. "And here you are."

"What's going to happen to Izzy? She has no parents now." Lily looked as though she wanted to weep for the poor girl.

"We have someone at the ranch who takes in orphans. She's a sweet woman with a big heart. In fact, Smitty is sweet on her. But if another family steps up and wants to take her that would be nice too."

"Any family?"

"Of course not. There are people out there looking for free labor, so I'd have to look at it from all angles. For now, would you mind watching over her? We still have no idea why her parents were targeted."

Lily frowned and tilted her head. "You don't think the Landsters were the reason we were attacked by that other wagon train do you?"

He stared at her for a moment then nodded. "You may be onto something. I've had a feeling something was off with them. They kept changing accents. I'm going to go through their wagon in the morning. "I'll help get Izzy settled into bed and leave you two."

"Where will you sleep?"

Her question warmed him. "Somewhere that I can still keep an eye on you. Don't worry we'll have guards posted." He lay Izzy down on a bed of blankets and turned to leave. He felt a tug on his sleeve and turned toward Lily.

She reached out and pulled his head down so she could kiss him. A jolt went through him as her lips covered his. Desire replaced his surprise, and he deepened the kiss. When they drew apart, he was breathless and he couldn't take his eyes off her. She seemed pleased with herself.

"Good night, Lily." He didn't wait for an answer. He just climbed out into the pouring rain with a big ole grin on his face.

He came face to face with Owen who was smiling. "Jed, you do know that with the lamp lit you cast a shadow everyone can see. That was some kiss."

Jed gave him a quick glare, and Owen stopped smiling.

"Keep watch for a bit. I want to go talk to Smitty."

"You got it."

Jed gave him a quick nod and trudged through the numerous puddles. It was going to be hard work when they left. The wagon wheels were mired in the mud.

Smitty had a fire going under a high tarp. He handed Jed a cup of coffee the minute he ducked under it. Then he subjected Jed to a long, hard stare. "I don't think that wagon train that attacked us was because of Lily. I never did think that. I think they were after whatever the Landsters have or had in their wagon. I'm not sure if the killer had enough time to get what he wanted."

Water poured off Jed's hat when he took it off. He sat down next to the fire and rubbed his hand over his face. As he sipped his coffee, he nodded. "Lily thinks the same thing, and it would make sense if we knew what they wanted. Someone with money must be behind all this. It would have taken some doing to get the wagons full of men to come out near us. I bet the man tonight was a hired gun. We might never know now that the Landsters are dead."

"I was thinking that too. Little Izzy is welcome to come live at the ranch with Lynn. My life had been simple but falling for Lynn has put a whole new spin on things."

"You'll get it all worked out."

"It'll take some doing, but I will."

LILY LAY with Izzy in her arms. It was morning, and still it poured. The sound of the rain against the canvas was oddly comforting. Jed with his weather prediction was right. She smiled. The look on his face of happy surprise when she'd kissed him warmed her. There was something about Jed Todd that had her acting like a schoolgirl.

Izzy stirred and when she opened her eyes they widened. She sat up and looked around and then hung her head. "They're dead," she said in a toneless voice. She sighed loudly and stared out at the rain.

"I'm so sorry, Izzy."

Izzy nodded. She suddenly seemed beyond seven years old. She turned and stared at Lily. "You are the one who survived the attempts on your life? You are the one who survived the Sioux?"

"Yes—"

"You will now protect me."

Lily furrowed her brow. It was more of a command than a question or even a request. "Protect you from what?"

"I must speak with Mr. Todd immediately." Izzy wasn't as calm as she portrayed. Her hands shook.

Lily nodded and got dressed. She put a shawl over her head and was ready to climb out of the wagon when she almost bumped into Jed.

A grin spread over his face. "Good morning."

"I was just about to come find you."

His brow cocked. "Any particular reason?"

Her face heated. "Izzy wants to talk to you. It seems rather urgent."

He nodded. "Let me set up a tarp outside here and we can talk. If I come in there now, your wagon will be nothing but mud. Give me a few minutes."

She nodded and sat back down inside her wagon. "Jed is—"

"Yes, I heard. I will need to take you both into confidence."

Lily gazed at Izzy. "How old are you?"

"I shall be eleven in a month's time."

"I thought you were seven."

Izzy nodded. "You were supposed to believe it. Things are not what they seem, and I'll need you and Mr. Todd to help me."

"Hello in there!" A male voice said.

"We brought you coffee." Lily recognized Jill's voice. The man with her must be the reverend.

Lily poked her head out of the wagon. "How kind of you. We're not quite dressed for visiting just yet."

The reverend handed her the tin mugs with a hard, unwavering stare. Then Jill handed her the pot.

"Well, thank you. I'll see that you get your pot and cups back." Lily sat back down in the wagon and began to pour coffee into a cup.

"Don't drink it!" Izzy said shaking her head.

"Why not?"

"It might be poisoned. Please just wait until after I talk to you and Mr. Todd."

What in the world was going on? "Of course. We can wait. There'll probably be a funeral for your parents today. You don't have to go. It's not unusual for people to be too distraught to attend."

Izzy simply nodded.

They waited in silence for Jed to get back. Lily kept playing different scenarios in her head as to what was going on, but her imagination wasn't wild enough. When the tarp was erected and a small fire was going, Jed grabbed a few crates from the back of the wagon. Rex stopped by and handed Lily a change of clothes for Izzy.

When they were all set, they climbed out of the wagon and sat on the crates. Jed went back into the wagon, grabbed two blankets, and wrapped them around Lily and Izzy's shoulders. He then put on a pot of coffee.

"Now, what is this all about?" he asked.

Izzy scanned the area. "What I have to tell you must remain a secret. My life depends on it. Obviously, someone knows my secret." She took a deep breath. "I will tell you the story but first I must get to the wagon to get proof of my birthright."

"Owen is guarding your wagon," Jed told her.

Izzy shook her head. "Edward and Joanne are not my parents. They were to get me to Oregon and look after me. I know this sounds farfetched, but I am the only child of Henry Fitzjames, third Duke of Albemarle and the Duchess Caroline Fitzjames. My father's greedy younger brother had men try to kill us all. They succeeded in the killing of my parents. Most people think me dead too, and it worked. I was able to get here to America with no problems. I fear that the attack by the other wagon train was against me." She stopped and nodded to Lily. "I'm sorry you took the brunt of the blame for it."

Jed poured the coffee and handed them each a cup. Izzy hesitated so Lily drank first. "You're afraid of being poisoned."

"Yes, with all the treachery and killings I can't help but be cautious. My parents entrusted me to the Landsters before they were killed and then I was immediately whisked away to America. We figured no one would look for me among people bound for Oregon." A tear spilled down her face.

"I'm so sorry, Izzy." Jed said. "What can I do to help?"

"First of all, I need Lily here to be my protector. I've never seen such a heroic woman in my life. We must keep our eyes open. The man who shot down the Landsters was an assassin. I pretended to be dead. I will remain inside the wagon for a while, and I want three graves dug. Two for today for all the travelers to see and then a third tonight for whoever is watching. They must believe I'm dead. Then we watch and wait. I'm sure there are people on the train that know who I am."

Jed nodded. "Were there any suspects?"

"At first we thought that Garber and Wanda were play acting to hate you, Lily, but were really targeting me. Edward followed them a few times. But they are just crazed lovers who want to do you harm."

CRAZED LOVERS? How strange to hear those words from a young child. Lily looked into Izzy's eyes and saw a wealth of knowledge as though she was an old soul. She probably had to grow up way too soon. But her information must be wrong. Garber tried to rape Lily and he was adamant about never marrying Wanda.

"Where in the wagon are your documents?" Jed asked.

Lily looked around again and leaned over toward Jed. She whispered to him and he nodded.

"I'll send Rex over to sit with you while I go to your wagon, Izzy. You're in good hands." He nodded to Lily.

Lily watched him disappear into the pouring rain. She grabbed the coffee the Callen's had brought over and dumped it out. She dreaded the thought of having to return the pot and cups to the Reverend and his sister. They wanted something. She'd never seen them give anyone anything.

Sure enough, they came out of the foggy rain. Lily tried to read their faces. Were they surprised she was still alive? Maybe the poisoning theory was a bit dramatic.

"I haven't had a chance to wash out the pot I'm afraid," Lily said. She handed to pot and cups to Jill, expecting them to leave, but to her surprise, they sat down at the fire.

"I feel ill." Izzy immediately climbed into the wagon and Rex's hand was on the handle of his gun.

The reverend took a Bible from beneath his coat and held it with two hands. "We're here on God's work. We don't think this is the right place for Izzy to be. She needs to be with people who can teach her right from wrong. Someone with an untarnished reputation."

Lily's jaw tightened as she stared him down. *Now he has a Bible*.

"Surely, you can understand," Jill said.

Lily shook her head. "No I don't understand how you two are supposed to be doing God's work? Doesn't God accept everyone? Izzy is staying with me."

Even in the rain, a crowd gathered, and when she panned it, Lily saw mostly frowns and glares directed toward her. Her heart sank. What was she supposed to do?

"I suggest you all just move away," Rex growled.

Lily's stomach clenched when no one backed away. They were finally going to try to lynch her. She wished she could kiss Jed one more time.

Rex pulled his gun and fired into the air. "I said move along."

Lily stood and put her back against the wagon. They'd have to go through her to get to Izzy, though it wasn't Izzy all of them wanted. "Izzy isn't doing so well. I fear she might be dying, so please just leave."

People stopped advancing. They glanced at one another and then most walked away. Of course, Garber and Wanda were still there.

Jed came running with his gun drawn. "What is going on here?" He glared at Wanda, Garber and the Cullens. "Izzy needs rest. She just lost her parents. You should be ashamed of yourselves."

Jill stood and put her hands on her hips. "I think it's you who is wrong, Jed. We've looked the other way about your relationship with Lily. Improper isn't a strong enough word for what you two have been doing every night. You will not fill that girl's mind with such filth."

Lily's mouth dropped open. What happened to the meek and mild Jill? Maybe Izzy was right and they were a danger to her. It was almost too much to take in. Jed sent her a reassuring look and she calmed a bit.

"We're leaving in the morning. Go back to your wagons and try to stay warm and dry. Smitty has a big fire going for all to share. Now go!"

The reverend stood, put his Bible back under his coat. "This is not the last of it. Izzy will be living with my sister and I as soon as she's well. I'm sure I'll have the support of the whole wagon train. We might have paid you to guide us but it doesn't mean we can't just go our own way without you. I have a guidebook so I'm sure I could lead. Come, Jill, let us go pray for Izzy's soul."

As they walked away, Jed turned toward Wanda and Garber. "Well, do you have something you want to say?"

Garber took a step forward. "Wanda and I are getting married and we want to raise the girl, right and proper. We'll be back tomorrow after we are married." He took Wanda's hand and they were soon swallowed by the fog.

A chill raced across Lily's skin. "They are going to take her and I don't think we'll be able to stop them."

Jed took a few strides toward her until they were toe to toe. "The reverend couldn't find his way out of a forest of only two trees."

"What about Garber and Wanda? Some people actually like them."

Jed sighed. "I know. Listen, get into the wagon. I'll join you after I take off my boots. I need to look at all the documents I found. And talk to Izzy some more."

She nodded and climbed into the wagon taking up as little space as she could. It was a tight fit with her and Izzy. Somehow, Jed would have to squeeze in.

CHAPTER EIGHT

The accommodations were tight, and Jed shifted in the wagon. What he wouldn't give to stretch his cramping legs. They'd been in it for hours reading over all of the documents from the Landster wagon. It was simply amazing, the declarations and the seals from some higher ups in England. It wasn't something he knew much about or really cared about until now.

Izzy's claims were true and she was due a big inheritance. They had their rules and traditions as convoluted as they were.

"If I'm reading this right, no one is to know who you are for all your life unless your uncle is killed."

Izzy swallowed hard. "Yes, that's the plan."

Jed met Lily's gaze. The tears in her eyes tore at him.

"It looks as though Lily and I are to keep you safe. We don't want anyone else to know your secret. They have gone to great lengths to make sure you never get your inheritance."

Izzy nodded solemnly. "What makes it the hardest is you

don't know who the enemy is. People are so good at pretending. You two aren't as good."

Lily furrowed her brow. "I don't try to pretend to be something I'm not."

A slight smile graced Izzy's lips. "You love Jed, and he loves you back. It's there if you look."

Lily turned a beautiful shade of crimson. "We're good friends."

He tried to hide the smile that threatened to appear. "We need to protect Izzy."

"She'll stay with me. I can protect her," Lily said with fierceness in her voice.

"I know you can, but I don't think you can do it alone," Jed said as he gazed at her.

"I won't have to. You can sleep under the wagon at night." Lily nodded as if it was the final decision.

Jed shook his head. "I think you've forgotten about the Callens and Wanda and Garber. They plan to fight it out for Izzy."

"You two must marry," Izzy insisted. "Please, it's the only way." She stared at Lily then at Jed, with a pleading look in her eyes.

Jed blinked hard. He couldn't say no and risk hurting Lily, but marriage was a big step. Too big to be made in haste. "What do you think Lily? Truthfully, I would've liked to have courted you more, but we can't allow anyone to take her from us." His heart sank at the defeated expression on her face.

Lily got up and climbed out of the wagon. She was going to say no, he knew it.

"We'll be right outside," he said as he left the wagon. Lily sat at the fire staring into it. He knew she heard him but she didn't look up.

He sat down on a crate next to her and turned toward her. Her frown tore at him. He waited until she turned to gaze on him, and his answer was right there in her bleak expression.

"We'll figure something else out. You don't want to marry me. I can understand. You'll have your choice of single men once we reach Oregon. I don't want this to ruin our friendship, though."

She shook her head. "I will marry you, Jed Todd. My life has not been one full of choices, and I accept that. Izzy matters, not me and not you. My opportunities in life were extinguished the moment Chayton took me. I'm grateful that I didn't have to marry him. What I really want to do is get on a horse and ride across the prairie with the wind in my face and my hair whipping all around. But even that would have to come to an end." She took his hand. "I just don't want you to feel tied down to a woman like me."

He opened his mouth but she put a hand up to stop him.

"Let me have my say. You will lose friends, and you'll be shunned from certain circles. Any children we have, if we have, will be treated like outcasts. There is no denying it or changing it. I'm tainted and I'm not to be trusted, that's what people say. Even the so-called good people of the wagon train haven't had time or inclination to nod their heads at me in passing. Going to Oregon won't matter. Most of these people are going there too, and all it will take is for one of them to talk about my capture. I will do this for Izzy, but I want you to know once we are settled at your ranch and I know she is safe, I'm leaving."

"Just like that, you'd up and leave?"

She nodded. "I'll be doing you a favor. It may not seem so now but you'll see. I just want you to know you won't be tied to me forever. You'll be able to marry some nice woman and have friends and go to all the socials and events in town." Her voice died out at the last word and she glanced away.

His now-empty hand felt cold without her hand in his. He had no plans to let her go. None. Was it fair to marry her when she thinks she can just leave? Smitty would be the one to ask but he didn't have time for that.

They waited for nightfall and slipped Izzy into Smitty's wagon. Then he and Lily rode to the wagon train that was about three miles behind them, seeking the preacher traveling with that train. They'd met him when camped at Independence Rock, and he'd seemed a decent sort. There would be no flowers, or music. None of the niceties that women liked but they didn't have that luxury.

The preacher had just retired into his wagon when they arrived, but he readily agreed to get up and marry them. He didn't know who Lily was, and that made it easier for Jed to breathe. He smiled into her eyes as he said "I do," and he saw a flicker of love in her eyes as she repeated her vows. The kiss was a bit hasty, and then they were off.

They planned to spend the night in the same wagon so everyone would notice come morning that they'd been together.

Owen was there to take their horses when they returned. "We dug the third grave and wrapped up some bedding and buried it. I think we fooled anyone watching. I didn't feel any eyes upon me."

"Thanks Owen."

Hand in hand, Lily and Jed walked to their wagon. They both left their boots outside as they crawled in. It was still just as cramped but he was able to stretch his legs out this time. He'd been running on adrenaline all day, and he was suddenly exhausted, but he had a duty to perform.

"Do you want me to turn my back so you can undress?" he asked.

"Why would I want to undress?"

It was pitch black in the wagon but he could make out the outline of her. "To consummate the marriage of course."

Instead of lying down next to him, she sat and he could feel the heat of her gaze upon him. "Did I say something wrong? In order to make a marriage legal we have to, well you know."

"If we do or we don't, who would even know? It's not like they will look for blood on the sheets or anything. They think I've been with dozens of warriors. I'm tired, Jed."

"You don't like me do you?" Jed asked.

"Of course I do. I'm just not ready. I will be a wife to you in every way but that, for now. That's all right isn't it?"

He ran his hand over his face. "People will expect us to be sweet to each other. You know like newlyweds."

She laughed. "We are newlyweds. I'm looking forward to spending more time with you, Jed. There is no other man I would have picked to marry. Look, why don't we kiss each morning and then again each night. Let me get used to you."

It sounded reasonable enough. "Fine, my new wife. Come lay down next to me, and let me hold you. Would that be acceptable?"

She lay next to him and readily went into his arms. "This is what kept me alive. I used to imagine that you were holding me at night, but my imagination never made me feel so good or so safe. Good night."

He lay there for a long time after she fell asleep thinking about his missed goodnight kiss.

"OH MY!"

"I told you she was a hussy!"

"Poor Jed, she finally enticed him."

Jed groaned as she sat up.

"They know," Lily whispered.

"That was the plan." Jed stretched his arms above his head. "We knew it was coming."

Lily quickly re-braided her hair and picked up her shawl. "We might as well get this over with." She pinched her cheeks.

"What'd you do that for?"

"I'm the blushing bride." She laughed lightly as he grinned.

He got out first, pulled his boots on and then held up his arms for Lily. She readily put her hands on his shoulders as he lifted her down. He swooped in fast and kissed her. He wasn't going to miss another kiss.

"What is the meaning of this?" Reverend Callan asked as he stepped in front of the crowd. He had a gleam of triumph in his eyes.

Jed smiled at Lily and put his arm around her shoulders, pulling her close to his side. "I'd like to introduce you to Mrs. Jed Todd."

He knew there wouldn't be many to congratulate him but the angry murmurs took him by surprise.

A vein on the reverend's forehead seemed to enlarge, and they could see it pulse. "Bedding a woman does not make her your wife. It makes her a whore!"

Jed stepped away from Lily and walked over to the reverend. "We went to the preacher in the wagon train behind us and got married last night. I knew you'd give us trouble about getting married, and frankly I don't need your approval or your opinion." He turned toward the gathering crowd. "That goes for all of you. I expect you to respect my wife and show her every kindness."

Smitty and Izzy stepped through the crowd. Izzy ran toward Lily and hugged her. "I'm so happy for you!"

Smitty patted Jed on the back and then shook his hand. "You made a good choice, Jed. It's a good match." He turned and hugged Lily. "Welcome to the family."

Lily smiled as she hugged Smitty. "Thank you. The first thing we are doing is adopting Izzy. She'll be traveling with us."

Garber pushed his way to the front. "Sorry, but Wanda and I have first claim on that girl." His eyes flashed in anger.

Jed shook his head. "A *claim* on her? That girl? Her name is Izzy and she has a right to be treated with love."

Wanda joined Garber. "What? She's ours!"

"Why?" Lily asked. "Why do you want her? I don't recall you ever talking to her or her parents."

Wanda's face turned a deep shade of red. "We have rights too, you know."

"Why doesn't anyone ask me?" Izzy asked in a loud and clear voice.

"You're a child," the reverend said.

"I am old enough to know my mind. I'm small for my age, but I can make my own decisions. I am going to live with Lily and Jed. I always fancied being a cowgirl."

Garber laughed. "There are only cowboys. It just shows you're a kid."

The look she gave him astonished Jed. It was a haughty, cutting look that brooked no challenge.

"I said I will live with Lily and Jed. They are both admirable people. They are well skilled in the art of living outdoors, and I feel safe with them. This discussion is over." She took Jed's hand in one hand and Lily's in another. "This is my family now."

The reverend cleared his voice. "No. Even though you married, I couldn't in clear conscience allow you to raise Izzy. My sister and I are above reproach, and we will take Izzy into our care." He put his hand out. "Come, Izzy."

Izzy tightly squeezed Jed's hand. "You have no right."

Jed patted her hand before he let go. "Izzy stays with me. Anyone who doesn't like it is free to go it alone. Getting out of this mud is going to be hard work."

Winston Richards shouldered his way to the front. "We stay an extra day or two until it dries. That's the only thing that makes sense." He shook his head at Jed. "Are you sure you've made this trip before?"

As much as he wanted to haul off and punch Winston, Jed restrained himself. "It might sound like a good idea, but as the mud hardens it holds tight to the wheels and it takes forever to dig out. It's best to get going as soon as we can. We'll be pushing wagons that get stuck—and they will get stuck—so everyone stay alert as you drive. If your wives can drive, let them. We'll need all the muscle we can get to push these wagons."

Winston puffed out his chest. "So, either way it's a lot of work. I know if I'm walking I want dry dirt under my feet."

Jed took a deep breath and let it out slowly. "I don't have time to debate with you, Winston. Either you're coming with us or you'll be left behind. I'm the wagon master, not a babysitter." Jed panned the crowd. "We leave in an hour. Have enough food and drink ready, we're not stopping for the nooning. It'll just be a waste of time as we'll all get stuck again. Anyone who doesn't help, doesn't get helped."

There was much grumbling, but Jed just shook it off. He wouldn't be surprised if they all followed. No one wanted to be on the trail alone. It was a recipe for disaster. He saw the wide-eyed expressions on both Lily and Izzy's faces and smiled. "Let's get you two ready to go. You'll want to shorten your skirts a bit more so you don't get weighed down by caked mud. Now once we get you going, don't stop. The trail up ahead is wide enough to steer around a stuck wagon, just keep going. Stopping makes for a better chance for the wheels to get bogged down.

Lily nodded and smiled. "We'll be fine. I know what to do."

Her smile was enchanting and his gaze lingered on her soft pink lips. He stepped forward, cradled her cheek in his palm, and kissed her sweet lips. Every kiss with her made his heart soar. He wanted to undo her hair and bury his hands in its silky blondness. Someday, he promised himself.

———

HER FACE GREW warm as he kissed her. It was like a home-coming each time, and she wanted to lose herself in his kisses. She couldn't help the wide smile on her face as they drew apart.

"Go, I got this. I'll keep her safe."

"Keep both of you safe." He walked away without looking back. He immediately had to help one of the families out.

"He's as handsome as a prince," Izzy said. Then she shook her head. "I take that back, I've seen some ugly princes in my time. I'm so glad you married him. I know you did it for me, and I hope you're not upset."

Lily put her arm around Izzy's shoulder. "I'm not the least bit upset. Now let's get ready. I have most things organized."

It was as hard as Jed predicted. Each wagon had to be pushed out of the ruts they were in and if they didn't keep going, they just got stuck again. It was a long hard day of trying to navigate around stuck wagons, but once they got Lily started, she was successful in not getting stuck again. That was a blessing. She wasn't sure if anyone besides Jed and his men would help.

Izzy was a very bright girl, so much older than her years.

Indian girls were that way too. Maybe it was because they both had to be smart to survive. She promised to show Izzy how to protect herself. That meant teaching her how to fight with a knife. Lily hoped that Jed approved. It was a whole different world out here.

She remembered the hopes and dreams her parents had when they started out on the Oregon Trail. Her father had wanderlust and there was something inside him that drove him to sell the farm and load up his wife and daughter in a wagon. Unfortunately, none of them had made it to Oregon. She would though, she vowed.

"Lily?" Izzy asked. "Do you think it cold or unnatural even that I'm not overcome with grief that the Landsters are dead? Is there something wrong with me? We've buried a few so far on this trek and I always see weeping and fainting."

"Were you close to them? Did you love them?"

"Not really, they were just caretakers. They treated me like a noble they weren't to touch. They were nice in their way and always very respectful towards me. They didn't want to come to America, but they knew their duty. I always felt bad about that."

Lily nodded. "The only thing I know is that we are each different. No two people mourn alike or love alike. Others expect you to act a certain way throughout your life. Everyone's life experience is vastly different. Look at you and me. I was captured by Indians and you escaped from England. We have nothing in common but I feel as though you understand me more than most. I used to be the type of girl who wept at funerals and smiled at weddings. Now I can only try to remain emotionless in front of others. I learned it from the Indians. You never want to allow your enemy to know what you're thinking. I'm sorry, I'm rambling."

Izzy reached out and patted Lily's shoulder. "I was taught

that also. Smile even though you're in pain, be friendly even though you want to slit their throats."

Lily laughed. "Don't let others hear you say anything about throat slitting, they'll think I put the idea in your head. Looks like we're slowing down. I bet we'll be circling the wagons soon."

CHAPTER NINE

*T*hree weeks later, they all stood around a tree waiting for Garber to be hanged. Jed had gone hunting, and Garber had stabbed Lily once again. The crowd was hostile, and while they wanted to kill Garber, Lily felt just as much animosity directed toward her.

This time Garber had climbed into her wagon as she drove, snuck up on her, and stabbed her in the back.

Lily screamed as searing agony ricocheted through her. Izzy stared, eyes wide, and then she also began shrieking. Pushing Izzy down on the floor and holding her with one hand, Lily drew her knife. Then she jumped up and lashed out at Garber. He dodged but she expected the move and was there with her knife. She cut him pretty bad, and blood spurted from a wound in his upper chest. He curled his lip back and lunged, and again she anticipated his move and met it with her knife. Then she switched hands and jammed the knife into the base of his neck. More blood flowed, but the wound wasn't bad enough to kill him. Howling, he leaped out of the wagon and stumbled away. Lily grabbed the reins and stopped the oxen. This had gone on long enough.

She quickly jumped down off the wagon, still holding her knife. The pain of Garber's knife stuck in her back was excruciating. The rest of the wagon train stopped, and a crowd gathered. They glanced from her to Garber and immediately found her at fault. Her heart pounded out of her chest. They'd all been waiting for this to happen.

"He stabbed me first. He climbed into the back of the wagon and stabbed me in the back again, like the coward he is!"

The looks of suspicion shifted toward Garber.

"Smitty," called Lily.

He made his way through the crowd. "I'm here, darlin'."

Fighting back tears, she presented her back to him. "Can you get this out of me?"

A collective gasp whooshed through the crowd. Everyone knew Garber's distinctive knife, with the carving of an elk on its handle.

"Let's get you sitting down," Smitty said as he guided her back to her wagon. "Is Izzy safe?"

"I pushed her down onto the floor when it happened."

Izzy popped her head out of the wagon. "I'm fine, thanks to Lily." She jumped down. "What can I do to help?"

"Can you start a fire?" Before she could answer, Rex was by their side.

"I got it. Lily will need someone to hold her hand when you take out that knife."

Lily watched Smitty and Rex exchanged worried glances.

Owen came running with medical supplies and a bottle. He set the bag down next to Smitty, then he opened the bottle. "Here, drink this."

Lily grabbed the offered bottle and smelled the contents. "Whiskey?"

"It's going to be painful, Lily. I'm not sure if stitching it will be enough." She watched as Smitty put a knife blade in the fire.

"You're going to have to burn the wound shut aren't you?"

Smitty nodded. "Drink up."

Lily did as she was told and drank some of the fiery liquid. She coughed as it burned its way down her throat.

"Best drink some more," Smitty advised.

She made a face and then took another long swig. This time her stomach wanted to rebel.

"Rex, I'm going to need you to hold her still."

Smitty cut the back of her dress from the collar to the waist. She held the dress to her front to retain her modesty. There was sympathy in Izzy's eyes. They gave Lily a stick to bite down on, and she tensed her body waiting for it.

It hurt when Smitty touched the knife. It was going to be bad when he pulled it out. She bit down hard on the stick and tried to hold in her screams as he eased the knife from her body. Finally, it was out and she could feel the blood pouring down her back.

"Just like I thought. I'll have to cauterize it," Smitty said grimly.

She closed her eyes and bit down onto the stick until it broke as the fiery hot blade of the knife was pressed against her skin. She screamed as the awful smell of burning flesh permeated the air. She wished she could pass out as she'd seen others do. Instead, she was wide awake and filled with pain. She hoped that Garber fared worse.

She'd waited for what seemed like hours for Jed to come back, but he hadn't yet. Smitty said he expected to meet up with the train about five miles from where they were now. She smoothed a hand over the skirt of her yellow dress. Thankfully, she'd mended it from the last time Garber had attacked her. It was no longer the color of buttercups but a kind of dirty, faded yellow, and the back bore bloodstains she hadn't been able to get out. The bodice on the green dress with the lavender collar that she'd been wearing earlier was likely ruined beyond repair, but she might be able to fashion a skirt out of it.

A commotion in the clearing drew her attention, and the next thing she knew, someone had fashioned a noose out of rope and swung it over a tree branch. Garber stared at it with horror in his eyes.

The crowd wanted blood and for once, it wasn't hers they were after. On another day, she might have fought their decision but she didn't have the strength. Hopefully Jed would return. They refused to listen to Smitty, Owen, or Rex. Even young Ricky Richards was holding a rifle on Garber.

"He's bleeding!" Wanda screamed. "He needs a doctor."

"He won't need to be patched up. He'll be dead soon enough!" A man in the crowd yelled.

The tension was high, and Lily feared Garber really would be hanged. Was Jed going to be too late? She listened for the reverend's voice but she never heard him protesting. In fact, she didn't even see him. As far as she was concerned, the reverend was good for nothing. She couldn't do anything about the situation, so she tried to calm herself. She was in a hell of her own. She grabbed the whiskey bottle and took another swig.

"Lily, spirits aren't good for you. Smitty said he'd make you some special tea," Izzy admonished.

"He's busy with his rifle right now. I don't remember having so much pain before. The whiskey helps a bit."

"I think I should help you back into the wagon. Sitting up is probably making it hurt worse."

"Perhaps, but I wouldn't miss this for the world. They all think that Indians are savages but look at their behavior. They are thirsty for Garber's blood."

The noose was placed over Garber's head, and Smitty fired his gun into the air. "That's a warning folks."

Rex hurried over with his pistol drawn and took the noose off Garber's head. He then took the rope and hogtied Garber. "He can't cause trouble now."

"He's still bleeding!" Wanda said, her voice hoarse.

"Bring him to my wagon. I'll get a fire started," Smitty said with a look of annoyance on his face.

Rex and Owen lifted Garber and dropped him on the ground near Smitty's wagon. Garber grunted in pain.

His pain gave Lily a bit of satisfaction. She saw dust kicking up on the horizon. It was probably Jed.

The incredulous expression on his face when he rode up on them made her giggle. She instantly covered her mouth. Maybe she'd had too much whiskey after all.

Jed jumped down from his horse, said something to Smitty and then he ran to her and hunched down. "How ya doin', honey?" He took her hand and stared into her eyes.

She smiled at him.

His brow furrowed as he looked from her to Izzy and back to her again. "You're soused!"

Lily hiccupped. "Perhaps a bit."

JED HELPED GET Lily into the wagon to rest. He hoped she didn't wake up with a huge headache. He grinned. She was a bit cute when drunk. She'd called him her handsome hero. He'd keep that to himself, though. She'd die of embarrassment if he told her.

His grin faded as he sat down next to the fire. He could have lost her today. Blasted Garber, why did he hate Lily so badly he'd tried to kill her? Jed suspected the other attempts on her life had been at Garber's hand.

He nodded as Owen when he approached him. "I heard you held your own today."

Owen nodded. "Rex and Smitty were of some help. Smitty wants to talk to you out of earshot."

Jed glanced at his wagon.

"Don't worry I'll guard both Lily and Izzy."

Jed nodded as he stood. He walked to the outside circle of the wagons. He stood still, making sure no one was watching him, then he headed into the woods.

Jed sat down on a fallen tree next to Smitty. "Thanks for taking care of Lily."

"She'll be fine. I think we have bigger problems than Garber hating Lily. He talks in his sleep and he's been mumbling about his big *payday*. Does any of that make sense to you?"

Jed sighed loudly. "Unfortunately it might. He wants Izzy dead. He was probably hired to kill her. Nothing is what it seems around here, and it's starting to get confusing."

"Why Izzy?"

Jed looked all around. He leaned in and whispered. "Izzy is due a big English inheritance and she has enemies who want her dead."

Smitty's jaw dropped. "What?"

"It sounds crazy but I have all the documentation. She was supposed to live her life with the Landsters. They were her protectors. I bet she has a price on her head."

Smitty nodded. "The reason for the third grave when the Landsters died. Makes sense now. What about Wanda?"

"She's just someone for Garber to hide behind. At least that's my theory."

Smitty stared into the fire for a bit before he replied. "Wanda doesn't know that. She thinks Garber loves her. Could it be that they just want Lily dead? Maybe they don't know about Izzy. Garber doesn't seem bright enough to pull off an assassination. He has trouble getting his boots on the right feet."

Jed stretched out his legs. "You could be right. Either way he's a danger to Lily if not to Izzy too."

Smitty shook his head. "Remember the good old days when we just had Indians and cattle rustlers to worry about? Lily sure has had more than her share of troubles."

"It would be easier if she was a wilting flower who hid in the wagon. She's the strongest woman I know, and I admire that about her, but she's had a couple of near misses. I'm surprised Garber got the jump on her. She usually has an uncanny feeling of danger."

Smitty grabbed his bag and drew out some dried leaves which he crushed into a mug. He then poured hot water into the same mug. "Here, give this to Lily."

"I will but she's sleeping. Should I wake her?"

Smitty laughed. "Listen."

Jed opened his mouth and then shut it again. He listened some more. "Oh no! Lily is singing and she sounds like a wounded steer." Jed took the cup from Smitty. "Cover your ears. I know I would if I didn't have to go make her stop."

Smitty's laugh started as a small rumble until it was loud and hearty. "Go on. I'll keep Garber for the night, and we can decide what to do in the morning."

Jed began to walk away, but he stopped and turned. "Thanks, Smitty."

Smitty averted his gaze. He always looked uncomfortable when he was thanked. "Get going."

Jed smiled and carried the tea to his wagon. His lips twitched when he spotted Lily. She sat on the wagon tailgate singing, reaching for the whiskey jug that Izzy was keeping out of her reach. Lily sang a song about a girl named Betsy, who had oxen or something. It was hard to make out.

She smiled brightly when she spotted Jed. "Howdy, Jed!

Izzy, this handsome man is my husband."

Izzy's eyes were so wide and her look was one of pleading. She must want Lily to stop singing too.

"Izzy, I got this if you'd like to lay down in the wagon and get some sleep," he suggested.

Relief spread over her tiny features, and she nodded.

Jed stood in front of Lily. "Come on darlin', let's dance."

Lily was a bit unsteady as she stood up and went into Jed's arms. Jed reached around her and put up the tailgate. "Good night, Izzy."

"I got stabbed today," Lily told him as she hung on to him.

"Yes, I know. You'll be fine."

"Garber is a piece of dirt. Just because he lost family to an Indian raid, he thinks I'm like that. I'm not, you know."

A slow grin spread across Jed's face. "I know you're not." He sat her down next to the fire and handed her the mug of Smitty's tea. "Drink this."

"Whiskey would be better."

His lips twitched with humor "Drink this first, then we'll see." He watched as she drank the tea down. She seemed calmer. "I'll grab what we need to sleep under the wagon."

Lily put her finger in front of her nose. "Shh!! Be quiet! Izzy is sleeping."

Jed wanted to laugh. If Izzy had been sleeping, she probably wasn't anymore. He climbed into the wagon and grabbed two oil cloths to put under them and enough quilts to keep them warm. He climbed back out and set to making them a place to sleep.

"Make sure you check for rocks. I know for a fact you never do. I don't want to hear you groaning and tossing and turning all night." Lily yawned. "I'm tired."

Smitty's tea was working. "Come love, let's get you into bed." He helped her under the wagon and got her all tucked in. "You'll be safe here."

"Come on and join me."

"I need to be on guard for both you and Izzy."

She shook her head and then stared at him. "I know other songs you know."

Jed groaned. "All right, move over." He lay there awake for most of the night. Lily had to lie on her stomach due to her wound, and she didn't move the whole time. Being so close to her was intoxicating, and while he enjoyed the closeness, he wasn't sure how'd she'd feel come morning.

LILY'S MOUTH felt dry and full of sand. The intense pain in her back brought it all back to her. The only good thing was lying with Jed. He was nice and warm on the damp night. What time was it? She couldn't get a good look at the sky to know.

What would they do with Garber? She'd noted the looks of disgust thrown at both of them. Garber had been behind all her troubles on this wagon train. Hate did awful things to people's minds. It had obviously poisoned Garber's. Wanda cared for him but why did they want Izzy? Those two weren't smart enough to be involved in Izzy's secret. Garber was driven by hate pure and simple.

The first notes of the sun started to play, and she gingerly crawled out from beneath the wagon. Reaching into the wagon, she grabbed her wrap and headed over to Smitty's fire. People might think her indecent with her nightgown on, but too bad for them.

Smitty smiled as she approached. "How's your head?"

She furrowed her brow. "I was stabbed in the back not hit in the head."

"Sit." He handed her a cup of coffee. "I thought with all the whiskey you drank you'd be feeling it this morning."

"My head is fine. I'm thirsty but other than that, only my back hurts. I made Jed clear the ground of rocks." She reached out and squeezed his hand. "Thank you for saving me yesterday. I know how hard it is to make a decision to burn the flesh and I also know the toll it takes to actually do it. You are a courageous man, Smitty."

Smitty's face turned red but the happy expression in his eyes warmed her.

"I'll find someone to drive your wagon so you can lay down inside—"

She shook her head. "That's not going to happen. I do need someone to drive the wagon but the ride will be too bumpy for me to lie down. It'll be easier if I walked."

Smitty gazed at her long and hard. "Knowing you you're probably right. Have Izzy walk with you in case you pass out."

Frowning she shrugged her shoulders. "That sounds like a fine idea." She looked up at the clouds. "What do you think? More rain?"

"No, not today." Her heart jumped at Jed's voice. "It'll be a fine day for a walk but you have to promise to let me know if you're in pain or if you tire."

"I will." She gave him a smile. "Smitty, what would you like me to do to help this morning?"

Jed stared at her. "I thought for sure after all your cater-wauling last night you'd be feeling poorly this morning."

"I'm right as rain. Well I do have some pain in my back but I've worked through pain before."

Jed squatted down in front of her. "Those days are over. You have a husband now. You can lean on me when you need to."

His kindness almost made her cry. "You are the sweetest man."

"Get me out of here!" Garber yelled from the wagon. "I demand you untie me!"

Jed and Smitty exchanged unpleasant looks. "Here we go," Jed muttered.

"Honey, go on back to camp and get dressed. Help Izzy and then come back for breakfast." When she hesitated, he added. "Please?"

Lily nodded and stood. "I'll be back in a bit. I forgot to ask. How much damage did I cause him?"

"Not as much as he did to you," Smitty answered, anger narrowing his eyes. "His knife was bigger."

"I'll be back."

Jed watched until she made it back to their wagon safely.

Smitty smiled. "You love that gal. It's written all over your face."

"Get me out of here!" Garber yelled.

"Keep your pants on. I'm coming," Smitty yelled back. "Jed you'd best help me. He's stronger than he looks."

Smitty pulled him out of the wagon and Garber hit the dirt with a loud thump. He lay there, hogtied.

Jed squared his shoulders. "First of all, I'll do what I can to keep you from hanging. Second, you'll need to hire someone to drive your wagon as you will ride tied up in the back."

Garber's face turned red. "You can't do that to me. I can't ride the rest of the way tied up!"

Smitty laughed. "Tied up, hanged, either way I don't care."

Jed and Smitty pulled Garber to the side of the wagon and tied him to the wagon wheel. Garber struggled the whole time.

"Makes no never mind to me if you eat or not Garber." Smitty shrugged. "It'll depend on your attitude."

By now most of the wagon train was up, and many people stared at Garber. But Jed didn't see much sympathy on their faces. "I'm going to check on Lily and Izzy," he told Smitty.

CHAPTER TEN

*I*t had been three weeks and Lily felt healthy and whole in both body and spirit. Walking with Izzy helped. She had so many stories of life at court and then exile in a country house. Izzy was very wise for her young years and she fit in well with her and Jed. They struggled up mountains and then down again. While she felt good, many of the travelers had taken sick and were weak.

Lily had offered to help drive wagons or have the lad who drove their wagon drive them, but no one would take a thing from her. The oxen were moving slower and more rests were required, but people still had possessions in their wagons they could do without.

Jed had gone from wagon to wagon again, insisting that they leave some of the furniture behind. He came back with his fists balled by his sides. "I told them I was leaving people behind that had heavy wagons."

"You already told them that," Lily said.

"Some didn't listen but were able to keep up." His lips thinned into a grim line, and he shook his head. "We'll never make it to Oregon before winter at this rate. Everyone needs to help with the oxen. These mountains have been hard on them." He took a deep breath. "You've been able to walk the whole way."

"I walked a great deal when I was living with the Indians. How are people set for food?"

"We almost never run out of food. We have the two extra wagons with just food in them for this part of the trail. We have about half of it left. I'm not worried about the food. I noticed a few didn't even take their oxen to water this evening."

"I'll go and help—"

Jed took his hat off and ran his fingers through his hair. "They won't allow you to help, and I can't have Izzy do it. I'll just round them up and lead them to the water before they decide to stampede to the stream." He gave her a weary smile. "It's the hardest part as far as I'm concerned. We lost three more people to scurvy. I'll have to get Owen and Rex to bury them."

She put her hand on his arm. "No journey is easy. We wouldn't have made it this far without you."

He put his hand over hers and gave it a quick squeeze. "Thank you. I'm off to empty wagons. Do they put things back into the wagons after I take them out? It's the only thing that would make any sense." He sighed. "I guess I'll find out."

Lily gazed at her husband as he walked away. He was such a good man and handsome too. Tara Scott was still eyeing him, but he didn't seem to notice. Lily warmed. Jed seemed to only have eyes for her.

She wished they could still sleep together but the nights in the mountains were cold and Jed insisted she sleep in the wagon with Izzy. Plus she could protect Izzy better if they were together. It could be no one else was coming for Izzy. Maybe the ruse of the three graves had worked after all.

Her back was healing nicely. She almost laughed. Poor

Garber had to walk behind Smitty's wagon with his hands tied. He never looked at Izzy but he sent a multitude of glares in her direction.

Since the last stabbing, she'd fallen into a routine of cooking for Izzy and Jed. They ate once in awhile with Smitty, but he was busy feeding hungry people. Many of the wives volunteered to help him. It was best she stay away.

"You look lost in thought," Izzy commented as she lay the fire.

Lily smiled. "I suppose I am. Jed said this is the hardest part of the trail but I feel good."

"That's because you know how to take care of yourself and the livestock. By the looks of some of the oxen, I'm not sure they'll last until morning."

"Jed is going to make sure they are all properly watered and fed. Some of the men are too weak, and they never showed their wives how to care for the oxen. But the good news is we're getting closer to the end of our journey."

They got the fire going and the coffee on. Next, she prepared the rabbit she'd caught that morning. The smell of cooking meat was heavenly and many watched her, but she knew they wouldn't take any if she offered. She'd hunted deer, pheasants, rabbits, and she'd caught a good amount of fish. If she happened to kill a big animal, she gave Smitty all the meat she didn't need. People were crazy. They ate it when Smitty offered it to them even though they knew where it had come from. Game was getting scarce, though. Well, at least her family would have rabbit to eat.

JED DIDN'T WANT to hear it anymore. This was the third time he'd taken the same furniture out of the Cooke wagon and each time they put it back. He sighed loudly. "Take a good look at your oxen! You should be ashamed of yourself, making them pull so much weight plus your wife," he yelled at David Cooke. "I *will* leave you behind. I'll draw you a map, so if you want to hand carry the furniture you'll know the way."

"The missus—"

"I don't give a plug nickel what she wants. Tomorrow I'd better see her walking at least for part of the day. Do you understand?"

David Cooke nodded and turned away.

Did these people have rocks for brains? Jed took a deep breath and went to the next wagon. There were many who had light wagons but they hadn't taken care of their oxen. He should have checked each night. They'd have the Blue Mountains behind them sometime tomorrow, and he knew a spot that had lush grass and plenty of water. They'd rest there for a few days.

After everyone had eaten their supper, Jed and Smitty got on their horses and drove the oxen to the small stream so they could drink. Some of the animals were bags of bones.

"It's my fault, Smitty. I should have seen how skinny the oxen were getting."

Smitty wiped his brow with his sleeve. "There are plenty that are fine. You can't take everything on your shoulders. It'll wear you to the nub."

"It's my job to get them to Oregon."

Smitty smiled. "We'll be in Oregon soon enough."

Jed shook his head. "Once we reach Oregon Territory, we still have almost five more days."

"The sooner the better. You have a house to build for your wife and daughter."

"Izzy?"

"You'd better make a proper claim to her before the

preacher ends up with her. He's still saying how Lily isn't a proper mother."

"I hear him every day. I think after we get these oxen all set, I'm going to make an announcement about Izzy."

Smitty spurred his horse downstream a bit where some of the oxen had gone. "Good idea!" he shouted over his shoulder.

Jed sat on Paint watching the livestock. Would Izzy welcome the announcement? What about Lily? He'd best make sure before he did anything.

As soon as he and Smitty were done he took care of Paint and then went in search of his wife. She was bent over turning over a piece of the rabbit she'd caught. She was one heck of a woman and one heck of a surprise. Both Lily and Izzy's faces were filled with smiles while they talked. His heart beat hard. It never occurred to him there would be any question about them becoming a family. He didn't like being unsure.

Lily glanced up and grinned when she spotted him. "Supper is almost ready. I bet you're hungry!"

He stepped closer to the fire. "I am." He waited for her to stand and then he was at a loss for words. He glanced from Lily to Izzy and back to Lily again.

"I don't know what's going on, cowboy so just spit it out," Lily said. Her smile was gone as though she expected bad news.

"I want to announce that Izzy is part of our family now. I want everyone to understand that she will be staying with us. That is, if you both agree." The silence that greeted him was unnerving.

Lily wiped her hands and smiled. "What a wonderful idea!"

Izzy's eyes welled up. "Thank you. I was hoping."

Jed opened his arms and hugged them both at once. Finally, they both stepped back. "I'm pleased you both agree."

THE THOUGHT of the announcement didn't agree with Lily. Her stomach was in knots. She wanted them to be a family but the rest of the people were bound to have a problem with it. Why did everything have to be so hard? She couldn't even sneeze without someone pointing a finger and blaming her for sickness. She tried to pretend it didn't bother her, but there were many times where their comments were arrows to her heart.

Izzy was the sweetest girl. Maybe it wasn't fair to bring her into a family where people hated the mother. This wasn't just making a commitment to Izzy; it was making one to Jed. She sometimes still wondered if she should just go off by herself so he could have a normal life.

"Honey, aren't you hungry?" Jed asked. His eyes were full of concern.

She summoned up what she hoped was a convincing smile. "I'm just a bit nervous is all." She turned to Izzy. "There are other people you could live with. I'm sure you noticed how people act toward me. I honestly thought surviving was like getting awarded the highest of achievements but it's like I'm branded as a nonperson instead. We love you, Izzy, but I want you to know what you're getting yourself into."

Izzy put her plate on the ground and hugged Lily. "I don't care what others think. I never have. I'd be honored to be part of your family."

Lily's heart lightened. "Let's do this before I lose my nerve."

Jed put his plate on the folded down tailgate. Then he pulled Lily into his arms. His eyes glittered in the firelight.

"I'm glad. It's the right move and not just to protect Izzy but because we've come to love her." He kissed her on her lips.

His kisses were what she thought of most days recently. His firm lips on hers, the way he cupped her cheek, and the look he gave her when he withdrew. It was though they were talking without saying a word. She could see into his heart at those moments and hopefully it was the same for him.

There was more, so much more to a marriage. She wasn't ignorant. There hadn't been much privacy living with the Sioux. During those times, she prayed that it would never happen to her but lately she'd been wondering and wanting. She wanted more closeness with Jed.

She and Jed held Izzy's hands between them when Jed made the announcement. A few people asked Izzy if this is what she wanted, and she answered yes. That satisfied more than half the crowd. Those left voiced their objections and not too nicely.

After the first disparaging remark, Jed asked Lily and Izzy to go back to the wagon. Lily gladly did. She thought she'd be used to it by now but it still hurt.

"Izzy, that is just a small example of how people will treat us."

Izzy smiled. "I don't care. I'm thrilled you and Jed wanted me as your daughter. My life keeps making so many twists and turns. This is a good turn." She kissed Lily on her cheek. "Don't worry I won't be sorry I chose you."

"You're so sweet, Izzy."

Izzy laughed lightly. "Thank you. I'm going to go to bed so you and Jed can talk." She started to climb into the wagon and then stopped. "Can I call you Mum and Jed Dad?"

Lily's throat thickened with emotion. "Yes, of course." She waited for Izzy to get into the wagon before she allowed the first tear of joy to fall.

She heard his footsteps and glanced up at Jed.

He held out his hand. "Rex will keep watch while we talk."

She clasped his hand and allowed him to lead her outside the circle of wagons, far beyond the firelight. They stopped near the stream.

Jed turned and put one finger under her chin and lifted until they were staring into each other's eyes. "Why are you crying? I know people can be cruel—"

"Happy tears."

"Happy tears?"

She nodded as she smiled. "Izzy asked to call me mum and you Dad. Her words touched me in a way I can't explain."

He visibly relaxed. "That is a reason to be happy. Who would have thought we'd have a daughter before we reached Oregon. Despite the naysayers, I'm a happy man. I love you, Lily."

Her heart filled to near bursting. "I love you too. I have for a very long time."

He pulled her into his arms and held her close. Then he kissed her cheek and jawline until he got to her neck. He sprinkled kisses over her as he unbuttoned the top few buttons to her dress. He kissed down farther, and then he stopped.

It was disappointing when he pulled away. His kisses were delicious, and she wanted more, much more. His touch made her body sing. She trembled as he buttoned her back up.

"I see the questions in your eyes, Lily. I want our first time to be special and not against some boulder in the dark woods. Our time will come. I want you so much it hurts, but you deserve respect."

"What if I said throw respect out the window?" She smiled.

"Trust me on this. It'll be a day you'll remember for the rest of your life and I want to get it right."

"When will it be right?" She touched his chest and felt his heart beating fast.

"I think at the ranch."

Disappointment filled her and she felt ashamed that she wanted him so much. "That will be just fine." She took her hand from him and for some reason she felt alone.

"I thought all men like to… you know." Thank goodness for the darkness. She hoped it hid her warming face.

"They do—"

"But not with their wives? Is that why there are so many soiled doves in the world?" She was just plain stupid. She didn't know the first thing about men or marriage. She could have sworn she'd heard married couples in their wagons.

"I have no idea how many soiled doves there are."

"What about where you live? Do you have one you like?"

He shook his head and grinned. "We are getting way off track. I wanted to kiss you and hold you and have you close to me. It seems like I'm always busy, and I wanted to steal time for just us. I wanted you to know how much I love you. I'd give you everything I own and then some. You are so very beautiful." He leaned down and kissed her again until her spine tingled.

She felt breathless when he finished. "I'm glad we had this time together. We'd best get back."

He took her hand and led her back to the wagon. "Sleep in the wagon with Izzy. I'm not sure if anyone got riled up enough to try to hurt either of you." He gave her a long lingering kiss before she climbed into the wagon.

She changed into her nightclothes and held her fingertips to her lips as joy filled her heart.

CHAPTER ELEVEN

*A*nother grueling day and two more deaths. Jed shook his head. Two boys were daring each other to run in front of the wagons and they both fell. It was always hard to bury the children. But they were finally in Oregon. They still had a good seven days to go but they'd make it. It will be a relief when he handed Garber off to the sheriff. Garber never shut up and he got on everyone's nerves. Quite frankly, he wondered why someone hadn't slit his throat by now.

They'd rested their oxen often over the last month, and everyone seemed to be in good shape. More and more people needed supplies from Smitty, but that was the reason he brought the food. He'd seen people who were starving on other trains. Many times, he'd seen pitifully thin dead bodies along the side of the trail. People hadn't had the strength to bury them.

Everyone on his train looked thinner but fitter. A few had bad coughs they couldn't shake but relief drivers were used when necessary. It all cut into his pay, but he'd rather make less and get his people to Oregon then cut corners and have too many deaths.

They would celebrate tonight. People would start to turn off the trail beginning tomorrow. Some already had land and families here and wouldn't have to go to the land office. He announced at the nooning that they were staying put for the rest of the day. It seemed to lifts everyone's spirits. He also wanted Lily in his arms as they danced.

Smitty immediately offered to keep Izzy by his side. Jed had to laugh.

"Anything to get out of dancing, Smitty."

"I'm not above using what I can. Let Rex and Owen dance with the single women." Smitty raised his eyebrows as his eyes twinkled.

Jed grinned. "Thank you for watching Izzy. It'll be a great help."

"That's me alright. Helpful."

Jed watched as everyone got busy taking baths and washing clothes. There wasn't much time to be idle on the trip. It hit him as he watched that this was his last trip. There was no way he wanted to be parted from Lily again. It jarred him a bit; he hadn't given it much thought.

"What's that grin for?" Smitty asked as he handed Jed a mug.

"I'm going to join my brothers and stay at the ranch year round. I'm going to miss the wagon train trips but I have good reason to want to build something of my own."

Smitty nodded. "Good choice. I plan to do the same. I have some business I have to attend to, but I'm hoping to make a certain woman my wife one of these days. She's all I've been thinking about the whole trip. Can you imagine me with a wife and a houseful of orphans?"

Smitty was already married, but Jed didn't say anything. It was a mystery Smitty never divulged. "Yes, I can imagine it, and I can imagine you being good at it. After all, you raised

Mike, Jed, and me. We weren't always easy to handle, and I do thank you."

"No mushy talk. It was an honor to raise my best friend's boys. I do have a few gray hairs due to you three, but it was worth it. We have a good ranch started, and I can't wait to see what we can make of it."

"I'd best see how Lily is. She still refuses to bathe in a river. I can't blame her but she'd carry the water herself and not bother to ask for help."

Smitty laughed. "Most men have the opposite problem. At least you won't be henpecked."

Jed strolled toward his wagon. Smitty was right, he'd never be henpecked. He'd made a good choice in Lily. He was just about to the wagon when Lily came running at full speed. He had to brace himself to catch her.

"Izzy is gone! She went to the river for a minute, and I can't find her anywhere." She took long deep breaths.

"Let's not panic yet. We'll look around first."

Lily looked doubtful but nodded. They split up and started to search.

Hours later, most had joined in but there was no sign of Izzy. The sun would be setting soon and Jed was out of ideas. There weren't any tracks leaving the camp, just to the river and back. Jed rode out anyway but found nothing.

Fingers began to point at Lily, and for the first time Jed was afraid for her. He had to stop her from searching and make her sit with Smitty. The look she gave him was scathing, but he refused to back down. He'd die if they lost her too.

It was one of the hardest things he'd ever done to go to her after dark without Izzy. Jed gently lifted her in his arms and carried her to their wagon. Tears streamed down her face, but she didn't utter a sound.

Jed undressed her and put her nightgown on. She didn't seem to care if he saw her undressed. He laid her down and then he lay next to her, holding her.

"I'm so sorry, Lily. I looked and I searched, but…"

She touched his shoulder. "Shh, my love. You've been through this before, and it's not fair you have to go through it again. Izzy is strong, and if it was Indians, she'll make it. If…if it was assassins again, we may never know what happened to her. I want to wail and scream at God, but I can only pray that He's watching over her. I've learned that not everything has an answer or a reason. I've learned that the ones you love can be taken from you in a heartbeat. For some reason, I don't think she's dead. I think she's close."

"I hope so. We'd best try to get some sleep so we can look some more tomorrow."

LILY WOKE TO ARGUING. Jed was already up, and she hurried to get dressed. It was barely dawn. *Did they find Izzy?* Her heart sank. No, it wouldn't be good news if they were fighting. Closing her eyes, she summoned all of her strength. She'd need every ounce.

She climbed out of the wagon and was surprised to see a few of the wagons ready to go. Where were they going? She had known they'd be splintering off now they were in Oregon, but the Reverend and his sister were supposed to be going to the end with them or so she'd been told.

She hurried to where Jed stood in front of the lead wagon. He immediately put his arm around her back holding the side of her waist. "Be ready to roll out of the way if it comes to it," he whispered.

She nodded slightly. "Where are they going?" she asked loudly. She wanted everyone to know that these people were just cutting and running. "Surely you want to keep looking for Izzy?" She stared at the reverend and tilted her head. "Isn't that what Christian duty is all about? Helping one another? I know you don't like me but certainly, you have compassion for Izzy. You wanted to raise her yourself."

The reverend never wavered. "We have commitments in town."

His sister Jill's face was so very white. She kept her eyes averted and her hands clasped in her lap. She seemed to stiffen at every word that was exchanged.

"Jill? Is this true? What about Izzy? You'd leave her lost in the wild?" Jill still didn't glance her way.

"Who else is going?" she asked Jed.

"Wanda and her brother and the Richards. If it were under different circumstances, I wouldn't blink twice, but something isn't right. The Richards just want to move on and Wanda and Dave want to do the same. Something isn't right."

Lily took a step forward. "Before you go Reverend Callen, could you lead us all in prayer that we find Izzy safe and sound?"

By now most of the camp was up and observing the confrontation.

"Let's all gather and pray shall we, Reverend?" Jed insisted.

Everyone gathered in the center of the remaining circle of wagons.

"Jill, join us too," Jed said.

As soon as everyone was focused on Jed and then the reverend, Lily stole into the Callen's wagon. Her heart beat faster and faster as she spotted a pile of blankets and grew certain Izzy was hidden beneath it.

As she pulled the heavy coverings aside, she spotted Izzy, bound and gagged, and struggling to breathe.

Lily's eyes filled with tears, but she hastily brushed them

away and unsheathed her knife. In seconds, she sliced through the rope bindings. She took the bandana out of Izzy's mouth, motioning for her to be quiet, and then she snuck her out of the wagon.

Izzy was a bit unsteady on her feet, so Lily took the girl's hand, and they went into the woods. As silently as they could, they circled around to their wagon but stayed hidden in the woods. Lily waited. It wasn't going to be pretty. Would the Callens continue on without Izzy?

Jed walked to the wagon, and she could see him searching the woods. She rustled a few branches to signal to him. He smiled and nodded and then left. Lily couldn't tell what was going on, but none of the wagons left.

People began yelling for Izzy; they were searching again. Maybe she should take Izzy further into the woods where they wouldn't be found. Just as she was about to put her plan into action, Rex showed up.

"Smitty is going to hang bedding to air outside his wagon. Once he has it set, we'll smuggle Izzy into his wagon and hide her. Be careful. I'm going to yell in a few minutes. Izzy can I rip off a piece of your dress? I want them to go in the opposite direction."

Lily didn't wait for an answer. She ripped a big strip off the bottom and handed it to Rex. "Thanks for this."

"I'm glad you've been found, Izzy." Rex turned and disappeared in the woods.

"Do you think this will work?" Izzy whispered.

"Yes, now let's go and be quiet."

They moved slowly through the woods and almost laughed when they heard Rex hollering about his discovery. All was set. Smitty made a small aisle between airing blankets for Izzy to get to his wagon. Lily gave her a big hug.

"You stay put. Smitty is one of the best men I know."

Izzy's eyes filled with unshed tears as she nodded and then hurried away.

Lily took a deep breath before she went back into the woods and joined in on the search. She spotted Jed and winked at him when he looked her way. He made his way to her side.

"Maybe you should be at our wagon in case she finds her own way back," he said nice and loud.

"I probably should. She needs to be safe." She started to walk back to camp when she found the Callens blocking her path.

"Where is she?" Kurt asked. She no longer thought of him as a reverend.

"In God's hands. Now if you'll excuse me."

Kurt grabbed her arm. "I'm not sure you know who you are dealing with. I have been given a job to do of the highest importance, and you keep getting in the way."

She pulled her knife and waved it in his face. "Kindly take your hand off of me."

Kurt glared at her and let her go. Then she was hit from the side with a branch. Jill? Lily rolled and was up on her feet in seconds. She held her knife in front of her. "I'm not afraid to use it. I could start with peeling your skin off while you're alive. Or… hmm I have so many choices. The Sioux are very creative people."

Jill's face turned red while Kurt's turned white. It was interesting to watch them trying to think.

"You wouldn't use that on us. The rest of the camp would have you hanged. Now drop it." Kurt attempted to pull a gun out from under his vest but he was too slow.

Lily kicked the gun from his hand and then had him on the ground. Jill tried to swing the branch at her again. Lily dodged the blow. Kurt crawled and got his gun but when he pulled the trigger Jill and Lily had switched positions and the next thing Lily knew, Jill was on the ground bleeding profusely. She was dead.

Before he could come at Lily, others were there, alerted by the sound of the gun. Owen wrestled the gun from Kurt, and Rex grabbed him by the scruff of the neck and dragged him to the middle of the camp.

Lily followed and watched in silence. It wasn't long before Jed was at her side taking her hand and leading her to Smitty's fire to get patched up. She'd never forget the look of fury on Jed's face as he left to deal with Kurt Callen.

"What do you think will happen, Smitty?" she asked.

"It was murder of Jill, plain and simple. There is only one action to take. I'm not surprised he wasn't a reverend. He was a strange one."

She briefly closed her eyes and then opened them again. "They're going to hang him, aren't they?"

Smitty shrugged. "That sounds about right. Not a word to anyone about Izzy or the reverend being a hired killer. Rex will stay behind and dig three graves and we'll leave markers with their names. If they thought she was still alive, they'll think her dead now. I hope she can live in peace."

"Wouldn't that be wonderful?" She grimaced as she reached for the coffee pot.

"Sit down and let me tend to you. You know if you're bad enough off I'm going to recommend you ride in my wagon for a while." He raised his brows. "If you catch my meaning."

Biting her tongue to keep from laughing almost didn't work. She'd always want Smitty to have her back but not for any clandestine type of thing. She wouldn't be able to keep a straight face. Suddenly, she smiled. "You made me forget myself."

After pouring them both coffee, he handed her a mug and then sat down. "What do you mean by that?"

"The Sioux taught me to remain expressionless no matter

140

what, and here I am trying to contain my laughter and smiling." Her smile widened. "That's a good thing, Smitty."

"See, I'm helpful in almost all things. Now let's get you bandaged up."

Smitty rehung the blankets for her privacy, and then he wrapped her ribs. "Not as bad as some of your injuries. Your arm is badly bruised too."

She waved him off. "Like you said, I've been worse."

"What's going on behind that blanket?" Jed joked.

"Join us," she replied.

Jed joined them, and his face was as far away from joking as one could get. "It's done. I've never had to hang anyone before. Not one person objected because he killed his sister." He studied her for a minute. "What about you? You could have been killed." He squatted down and took her hand. "How hurt are you?"

"Bruised ribs and arm. Nothing really."

Jed smiled deeply. "Only you would say those injuries are nothing." He sighed. "I'm lucky to have you."

Smitty discreetly left them alone, and Jed kissed her and his kiss was full of love. She could feel it and it moved her. It didn't matter if others liked her or not. He was her home. It had been such a hard road the last few years and she kept hoping that some light would shine through and it did. It did in a brightly huge way. It was as though the black clouds parted and the sun was shining down just for her.

"I'll be staying in Smitty's wagon until I'm better." She nodded toward the wagon.

Jed smiled. "I'll just go and make sure it's comfortable."

"Do so quietly." She grinned.

Lily waited outside while Jed was hugging Izzy. Not every man would take in a child, but her Jed had readily done so.

Jed climbed out and gently held Lily. "I don't want to let go of you." His voice was muffled.

"I feel the same. Maybe I could sleep in our wagon after all."

He leaned his forehead against hers. "I wish you could, but I'm still afraid for Izzy."

"I know you're right, but…"

"Our time will come." He helped her into the wagon.

CHAPTER TWELVE

The landmarks all looked familiar. One more day and they'd be right outside of town. Jed had sent Rex on up ahead to his ranch to let his brothers know he'd made it and he needed some help. Jed had talked to Lily about it and they decided to hide Izzy on the ranch for a few months so they could be sure no one else was looking for her. She'd be safe there.

Unfortunately, that meant almost a week of traveling in the wagon, and lily was not happy. He'd found that she could be as grouchy as a bear. A bear he could tame with kisses, though. It was just as well no one wanted to talk to Lily. That made it easier to hide Izzy.

Hopefully, he'd be able to spend a night alone with his wife soon. Maybe tonight he could get them a room in the hotel while Smitty guarded Izzy. Something stirred inside him. Then he frowned. That wouldn't be fair to Smitty. Maybe if they were only gone for a few hours and not the whole night…

Owen rode up next to him. "We're almost home. I want to

thank you for the confidence you've had in me this trip. We are going next spring, aren't we?"

Jed shook his head. "Owen, I think it's time for you and Rex to run things. I finally found Lily, and I don't want to be parted from her."

Owen frowned. "I'll talk to Rex. I can't believe all the Todd brothers have gone and got hitched. I remember the days when we all pledged that women weren't for us. I don't suppose Smitty?"

Jed shrugged. "He has Lynn Downing waiting for him. I have a feeling he's going to want to settle down. I could be wrong."

Jed rode up and down the train. "The land office will still be open when we get there," he told many of the folks. The relief on his fellow travelers' faces warmed him. They'd made it. They had lost a few, and that was always the sorrow of the Oregon Trail. He hoped they stuck it out and made lives for themselves. He'd seen too many people go back, and many had nothing waiting for them back home.

Oregon was a big territory with plenty of space to start a life. The relief and happiness would wear off when they got to their properties and realized the hard work wasn't behind them, it was just starting.

Winter would be hitting in a matter of months, and they needed to build shelter. There wasn't time to get a crop in before it snowed, but there was plenty of game if they hunted. All he could do was wish them the best of luck.

Buildings could be seen in the distance, and the people cheered. They'd circle one last time, and folks would make a mad dash into town to either get supplies or land or both. He always stayed that one last night before heading home. He'd considered every scenario he could think of, but he couldn't figure out how to be alone with Lily.

He wanted her all to himself before his family got ahold

of her and made her feel welcome. After that, who knew? The house was plenty big, but he didn't want people knowing his business. He smiled. He guessed his brothers went to bed to do the same thing.

Heck, had Eli and Amy had a boy or girl? He bet Cassandra was walking already if her daddy Mike allowed her to take a step. He seemed mighty protective. He wouldn't allow Jed to hold her unless he was seated. It would all work out.

Just as he'd expected, some circled while others just parked and went running to see if they could get the best land. He laughed as he rode to Smitty's wagon. "We're home."

Smitty's eyes twinkled. "Looks like you have a welcoming committee."

Jed frowned and looked toward town. There stood his entire family waving at him. "What do you suppose this is all about?"

"Don't care." Smitty shrugged. "I get to see Lynn that much sooner." He climbed down and hurried off. Jed had never seen him walk so fast in his life. Smitty grabbed Lynn and swung her up into the air before he soundly kissed her.

"Psst! I thought he was married." Lily whispered.

"And I told you that's his business. He's not a scoundrel. He's just a man with a big heart."

"Your family is here," she remarked.

"Every single one of them. It's strange."

"Don't you think you should see why they're here? Izzy and I will be fine here for a while."

"I'll be right back."

LILY WATCHED as he hugged and kissed his family. It made her long for her mother and father.

"Looks like a nice family. I'm a bit confused by Smitty's girl. Her kids are of all colors," Izzy said.

"She adopts children who have lost their parents along the Oregon Trail."

"That's good. People don't need to know who I am. Just another orphan."

Lily studied Izzy. "You'll be just fine. I've met Jed's brothers and Mike's wife Susan before I was captured. They were always so nice. Susan and my mother were good friends. Now me, I don't know if my being with the Sioux for two years makes a difference or not. I'd say not, but you never know."

Izzy giggled. "Look! They're running over here to see you, so I think that answers your question."

Lily's stomach clenched as her mouth went dry. If they rejected her in any way, she'd die.

"Stay in the wagon, Izzy."

Izzy nodded, and Lily climbed down ready to face them down. Poor Jed. But she wouldn't make him choose between his family and her. His family was too good to pass up.

Susan had tears in her big blue eyes and she pulled Lily into her arms. Susan was very pregnant and hugging was a bit awkward. "Look at you! Oh my, you're so beautiful. I wish your mother could be here to see you safe."

"It's good to be here."

Mike was right behind his wife carrying a little girl with dark hair and blue eyes like her daddy's. "I hear we're related now." He smiled and kissed her cheek. "This is your niece Cassandra."

"Jed's told me all about her. She's adorable."

Eli waited his turn and picked her up, twirling her around before he kissed her on the cheek and then set her down. "You are a sight for sore eyes. I'm ecstatic you were found. Jed looked for you everywhere."

"I'm glad I was found too."

"Oh, where are my manners? Lily, this is my wife Amy and our son Grant."

Amy had her hands full, but she smiled. "I've heard a lot about you. Welcome."

Jed put her arm around Lily and smiled. "They all came to town to see you."

She glanced up at Jed wondering if they were putting on a good face accepting her or if…?

He gave her shoulder a light squeeze. "What you see is what you get with the Todds."

She hadn't realized how tense she'd been until she began to relax.

Smitty walked toward them with Lynn and her crew of kids.

"Looks like there are a few more than when I left," Jed commented.

"There are," Mike said as he smiled.

"I heard there is an important package that needs to get to the ranch," Eli said. "Smitty mentioned you two hadn't had any privacy." His face turned red.

"I paid for a room for you at the hotel. It's available now," Mike said. "Eli and Smitty will take everyone home while I make sure the people from the train get settled. You two go ahead."

She looked at the ground, embarrassed. "Jed, could I talk to you?"

His brow furrowed but he followed her a few feet away from the rest. "What is it?"

"This might sound strange, but I don't want to use the hotel room. I want to be under the stars with you. It's the way I always dreamed it would be between us. Unless you prefer—"

He stepped back toward the group. "Change of plans.

We're taking one of the wagons and having one last night camping."

Mike laughed. "Well what are you waiting for?"

"Take good care of the package. Oh, and Smitty, don't forget to get the sheriff to take Garber off your hands. You know we never did figure out what his big payday was supposed to be."

Smitty rubbed the back of his neck. "I thought I told you. Wanda and her brother seem to be wealthy. Garber wanted to prove his love by getting rid of Lily. She scared Wanda I guess."

Lily joined Jed and took his hand. "Well now we don't have to worry about them."

Jed stared at her as he caressed her cheek. "Ready?"

She suddenly felt shy when she nodded. She didn't look back but climbed onto their wagon and smiled as they went in their own direction. They drove in silence but it was a good silence. A silence of relief, excitement, fear, and love. She enjoyed every minute of it.

Jed parked the wagon next to a stream and under a few trees.

"It's lovely here." The babbling of the stream along with the sound of the leaves as the cool air blew was calming. Birds sang as though they were welcoming them."

"I'll get a fire started so I can heat water for you."

"I wish I was brave enough to wash in the stream."

Jed shrugged. "It's a bit cold anyway. Now did you really mean under the stars or would you be more comfortable in the wagon?

She climbed down and took a few steps from the wagon where the trees didn't block the sky. "Here. Right here."

Jed built a fire close to the spot she indicated and when he had the water heated and ready he said he'd hold a blanket up for her privacy. She shook her head. I want us to bathe together and sleep together. I want to be your wife in all ways and I want to make you happy."

"You already make me happy, but let's get cleaned up, Mrs. Todd."

Lily didn't know what happiness really was until she lay in her husband's arms later that night. They looked up at the stars and she made endless wishes for them.

EPILOGUE

wo weeks later, Lily and Jed went for a walk in the moonlight. It was a heavenly sky with a full moon and plenty of stars. Happiness filled her, and she hoped it would never fade.

"Your family has been so welcoming. I feel like I belong, and I never thought I would have that. So many things have happened to me these last few years but I think I got my happy ending."

"We have a lot of hard work to do. I want to build our own house on the adjacent property and claim more land. I'm entitled to more since marrying you."

She elbowed him in his side. "So that's the real reason you married me. I knew there had to be a reason," she joked.

"A man has to look out for his future." He gave her one of his heart-stopping grins as he turned her to him. The grin faded as he leaned close and kissed her. It was a gentle, lingering kiss. When they parted, he gazed at her with hooded eyes.

She knew that look by now and was waiting for him to take her inside but he looked up at the sky instead.

"You know, this life is full of wonders. Some good and some not so good. The day you were taken changed my life... I grew up that day, and I realized I had feelings for you. You were so young..."

"I'm so glad you kept looking for me."

He took her into his arms and kissed her neck. "Ours was a love worth searching for."

ABOUT THE AUTHOR

Sexy Cowboys and the Women Who Love Them...
Finalist in the 2012 and 2015 RONE Awards.
Top Pick, Five Star Series from the Romance Review.
Kathleen Ball writes contemporary and historical western
romance with great emotion and
memorable characters. Her books are award winners and
have appeared on best sellers lists including: Amazon's Best
Seller's List, All Romance Ebooks, Bookstrand, Desert
Breeze Publishing and Secret Cravings Publishing Best
Sellers list. She is the recipient of eight Editor's Choice
Awards, and The Readers' Choice Award for Ryelee's
Cowboy.
Winner of the Lear diamond award Best Historical Novel-
Cinders' Bride
There's something about a cowboy

facebook.com/kathleenballwesternromance
twitter.com/kballauthor
instagram.com/author_kathleenball

So Many Roads to Choose

The Settlers

Greg

Juan

Scarlett

Mail Order Brides of Spring Water Books 1-3

Tattered Hearts

Shattered Trust

Glory's Groom

Mail Order Brides of Spring Water Books 4-6

Battered Souls

Faltered Beginnings

Fairer Than Any

Romance on the Oregon Trail Books 1-3

Cora's Courage

Luella's Longing

Dawn's Destiny

Romance on the Oregon Trail Books 4-5

Terra's Trial

Candle Glow and Mistletoe

The Kavanagh Brothers Books 1-3

Teagan: Cowboy Strong

Quinn: Cowboy Risk

Brogan: Cowboy Pride

Made in the USA
Monee, IL
06 January 2024

51316176R00095